Praise for Hillary Waugh:

"Really intelligent crime fiction, like really intelligent writing of any other kind is rare; but there can be no doubt that Hillary Waugh produces it. Every step of the police investigations he describes has been carefully plotted and cunningly calculated to keep just ahead of the experienced reader's speculations."

—*Times Literary Supplement*

"The thiller-writer Hillary Waugh is outstandingly good." —*Spectator*

Also by Hillary Waugh available from Carroll & Graf:

A Death in a Town

HILLARY WAUGH
Sleep Long, My Love

Carroll & Graf Publishers, Inc.
New York

First Carroll & Graf edition 1989
Reprinted by arrangement with the Ann Elmo Agency, Inc.

Carroll & Graf Publishers, Inc.
260 Fifth Avenue
New York, NY 10001

ISBN: 0-88184-552-3

Manufactured in the United States of America

PROLOGUE

It was ink black in the back bedroom of the little house, black and suffocatingly warm. With the shades down, the windows closed, and the heat up, he could feel the room pressing in on him, holding him, smothering him like a womb.

He couldn't see the naked girl in the bed beside him, but he could feel her, feel her head on his shoulder, her arm across his chest, her body against his. He stared up into the blackness, his right arm lightly around her, and wondered if she were asleep. He wondered if he'd waited long enough and because he wasn't sure, he hesitated to move. Slowly he turned his head toward the radium dial of the watch he'd set on the bedside table. He moved carefully, holding the rest of his body still, but his hair rustled on the pillow.

The woman raised her head. "Stay the night, Johnny," she whispered.

He turned back and stared again at the warm close darkness above. "You know I can't," he answered woodenly.

She struggled to one elbow and leaned over him. He could feel her warm breath in his face. "Come on, Johnny," she murmured. "The hell with anything else. What do you care?"

He pushed her aside firmly and sat up. He reached for his cigarettes and she came up too, throwing the covers back. He fumbled in the darkness, put a cigarette in his mouth and flicked his lighter. Her voluptuous body glowed pale orange in the flickering light, but he didn't look at her. He snapped the lighter shut, inhaled deeply, and blew out the smoke harshly. He swung his bare legs over the side and sat with his back to her. She moved in against him, one hand around his waist, the other on his shoulder, her head close to his. "Johnny, what's the matter? Everything's going to work out fine." She rubbed a finger lovingly over the mole on his right shoulder blade and he hated it. He wanted to lash out at her, to hit her, to make her stop, but he was careful to give no sign. Instead, he stood up and moved away from the bed. "That's just it, it won't work out," he said harshly.

He heard the springs creak and then she snapped on the table lamp at the other side. The room leaped into garish light, the black drawn shades, the chipped bureau, the tarnished silver-plate brush with her loose hairs in it, the messy bed, and the two wobbly bed tables. On the sheets her body looked large and ponderous in the glare. It had been a luscious body eight years before and it still was eye-catching now. She was a little heavier, a little fuller, but well proportioned. It was an admirable body for a thirty-year-old woman and there was a time when he had enjoyed seeing it, but that was before he came in conflict with her personality. Now her personality colored everything. Now it made her repulsive and he only wanted darkness.

"Turn off that light," he said, whirling on her so angrily that she obeyed almost by reflex. He took one more deep, fretting drag on the cigarette and the lamp snapped on again, this time to stay. She came across the bed, raising herself to her knees and putting her hands on her hips. There was a touch of fear in her voice. "What do you mean it won't work out?"

"Just that." He sat down again and stared at the floor. "It's no good. We might as well face it."

She swung off the bed quickly and stood in front of him. "You can't say that. It *will* work. I'm not going to let it not work!"

He looked up at her then and he couldn't keep the anger entirely out of his voice. "Will you grow up? You're not a child any more. I agreed to give it a try and we've tried it and it doesn't work."

"You agreed to try for three months. It's not even one month."

"I don't need three months."

Her voice rasped with sudden bitterness. "You didn't need one month, I'll bet. You had no intention of giving us a chance when you started. Your mind was made up before you began." She dropped to her knees then and put her hands on his arms. "Johnny, Johnny, please. Let's not fight. If you'd only do it right! If you'd tell your wife you're going on a trip and come stay with me, so we could really live together, so I could cook for you and keep house for you, so I could show you how much you need me! This isn't any good, just evenings, you coming in and going home again. This should be your home. I'm the girl you need, Johnny, not her—not your wife! We're the same kind of people. You know we are." She ducked her head to see into his lowered face. "Look at me, Johnny. Tell me you know I'm right."

He looked at her and his eyes were cold. He said, "Can't you know a man hates a clinging vine? Why do you have to hang on? Can't you tell when something is over?"

She sank back slowly, sitting on her ankles, dropping her hands to her lap. She met his eyes squarely, ignoring their look. "I'm not going to let you go, Johnny."

His mouth tightened. "What do you want out of me? Is it money? I know you quit your job. I'll give you money. I'll come and see you if you want."

She was losing him and she could sense it. He looked at her and didn't see her. She was naked and he didn't notice. She bit her lip and watched him puff jerkily on his cigarette. When he turned for the ash tray, she spoke. "I'll tell you what I want," she said evenly. "I want a father for my baby."

He started. "Your baby?"

She nodded. "I didn't want to tell you. I didn't want to hold it over you. But you forced me. You're going to have to marry me, Johnny."

He reached numbly and mashed out his cigarette, then hunched over, staring again at the floor. He heard her move, but he didn't look up. She came beside him on the bed, pressing against him, her face close to his ear, her hands stroking his shoulders. "It's all right, Johnny," she whispered. "You can get your divorce in Reno and I'll go out with you. I'll make you happy, Johnny. You see, if I don't—"

She kept on talking, but he had stopped listening. He had hoped against hope he would be able to discourage her. He had thought perhaps this month together would make her want to break it off. He had hoped there would be some other way to get her out of his life, but the baby queered it all.

Now he knew he would have to kill her.

Since it was vacation and he didn't have to drop his two little girls off at school, Raymond Watly, thirty-five-year-old real estate agent, didn't leave his home in Ashmun until eight-forty and didn't arrive at the Restlin Real Estate office in Stockford, Connecticut, until ten minutes of nine. The office, on Farnsworth Street, occupied the left half of the first floor of an old frame house. There was a plate-glass window with the name in gold letters, balanced by a matching window to a law office. A recessed door between opened into a dingy through hall from which both offices could be reached.

Mr. Watly, as was his custom, turned into the dirt drive beside the house and parked near the tumbledown shed in back. He entered the hall through the rear door and strode over the creaky planking to the office entrance, taking out his keys and whistling a tune. When he got there, he didn't put the key in the lock, but stopped and looked. The frosted pane in the door was broken. There was a hole in the glass as if someone had put a fist through it close to the knob. Cracks ran from the hole across the rest of the glass and, inside the office, fragments lay on the floor. Mr. Watly tested the door, but it was locked. He reached a gloved hand through the hole and saw he could turn the inside knob, but he withdrew his hand without touching it. He now used the key to let himself in, closing the door gently, touching only the frame. A quick look around showed him that the safe was intact and nothing seemed out of place, but the broken window was enough for Mr. Watly. He picked up the desk phone and dialed his boss, catching Mr. Restlin about to leave his home. He said, "Frank. You'd better get down here right away. It looks like somebody's broken in."

Mr. Restlin was there in five minutes, pulling in at the curb and scrambling out of his car almost simultaneously. Mr. Restlin was a bustling little man, a gray-haired gnomelike creature who had found real estate a more likely prospect than women and had married his business. The operation was a mistress of many facets. Not only did the Restlin Company act as agent in sales and renting, but in many cases acted as landlord, performing the service for its clients of managing their property and collecting their rents. In addition, Mr. Restlin was a landlord himself several times over, so there were few phases of real estate that the Restlin Company didn't handle. It was a company that had grown fat under his watchful eye and his concern over this threat to it was immense. He almost ran to Watly on the stoop saying, "What is it, Ray? They take anything?"

Watly tried to tell him he didn't know, because he hadn't touched anything, but Restlin was already past him and into the hall. There, he glared at the hole in the pane and the pieces of glass on the floor inside. He tested the knob on both sides of the door while Watly, hanging over him nervously, said, "I don't think you ought to touch anything, Frank. If it's robbery there might be fingerprints."

"I don't know what it is," Restlin said shortly, "but I'm going to call the police." He went to the phone without taking off his hat.

It was Sergeant T. C. Unger who took the call, but Sergeant Unger wasn't important enough for Mr. Restlin and it was relayed to Chief Fred C. Fellows in his small office back of the main desk. Fellows listened quietly to Restlin's expostulations and then said, "A broken window? What are we supposed to do about that, Mr. Restlin?"

"It's not just a broken window," Restlin snapped. "It's breaking and entering, that's what it is. It's burglary."

"What's missing?"

"I don't know yet. I haven't looked. You'll want to fingerprint, won't you?"

Fellows allowed that he might and said he'd send someone over and hung up with a sigh. He went to his door and gestured. "All right, Sid," he said to Detective Sergeant Sidney G. Wilks. "You'd better go over to Restlin Real Estate. He thinks he's been robbed."

Restlin's was only two blocks away in downtown Stockford and Detective Sergeant Wilks walked the distance in the biting, ten-degree cold. When he arrived on the scene, he found Frank Restlin on the stoop in a dither of excitement. "Look, look," the man said, half dragging the sergeant to the office door. "They stole all my leases. All my leases are gone."

Wilks stepped inside and looked around. The door of the small safe near the front window was swung wide, but it was to the large gray steel file cabinet against the opposite wall that Restlin was pointing. The middle drawer was open and some of its contents were piled on the floor.

"Your leases?" Wilks said in some surprise.

"All of them. I had them in there. The whole folder's gone. They've been stolen."

Wilks rubbed his cheek. "Any idea who'd want your leases?"

"How should I know? You're the policeman. You're supposed to tell me. Take fingerprints. Do something."

"In time, in time." Wilks sat down at the desk and took out a notebook. "Let's go about this systematically," he said. "Who found what and what's been touched?"

Watly, standing by, didn't have a chance to explain his part in it. Restlin did it for him. "Ray here found the broken window and he called me. I came down and called you. Then I opened the safe, but nobody'd touched that. I looked through the files while we were waiting for you, and that's when I found out the leases had been stolen."

"You keep the file cabinet locked?"

"No. I didn't see any point. The door's always locked." Restlin paced the floor as if he'd been wiped out. "I can't understand why anybody'd want my leases."

"You any idea, Mr. Watly?"

Watly shook his head. He was a tall, rather good-looking man, dark-haired, with a pale complexion, and he was calm about the whole thing. He sat on a corner of the desk watching his feverish employer. "I couldn't imagine why anybody'd want those leases. What good would they do them?"

"Take fingerprints," Restlin said. "He must have left some prints."

"He might have," Wilks agreed, "but with you opening everything, they're probably spoiled."

"I couldn't wait all day. You took so long. You should take prints anyway. He probably left others."

Wilks shrugged. "Maybe. I don't know that finding them would help us much."

"Why not? They'd point to the burglar, wouldn't they?"

"Only if we happened to have the burglar's on file. I rather imagine we don't." He stared musingly at the open file drawer. "You're sure nothing else was taken?"

"That's the only thing."

Wilks flipped his book shut and stood up. "I'd guess this wasn't done by a professional burglar, Mr. Restlin. This was somebody who wanted the leases, or one such lease. You have any other record of who's living where and for how long?"

"Yes, of course." Restlin crowded Wilks aside to get into the middle drawer of his desk. He pulled out a ledger. "This wasn't touched. Besides that, I can tell you everything about everybody, who's renting what, who owes what, when their leases expire." He tapped his head. "I've got it all right here. If somebody thinks I wouldn't know without the leases, that somebody has another think coming."

"Anybody owe you a lot of back rent? Anybody want to break a lease?"

"Hmmph. Well." He peered at the sergeant. "You think somebody's trying to do me out of something?"

Wilks said, "You have your tenants' signatures on anything other than the leases?"

"Well, on some of the applications—where they applied in writing."

"That wouldn't be binding in court, would it?"

"Well, what do you mean?"

"I mean if one of your tenants wanted to skip out, you wouldn't be able to sue him if you couldn't produce a lease, could you?"

"Then you think—" Restlin stopped. His small, wizened face got tight with rage. "Now who would it be? Who'd try a dirty trick like that?"

"You may find one of the birds who owes you money has flown the coop."

"Who owes us?" Restlin didn't trust his memory on that and dove for his ledger. Wilks went to the door and stooped to examine the brass knob. He reached up to turn on the overhead fluorescent lights and examined it again. "There're a couple of prints on the doorknob," he said. "Either of you touch it?"

Watly said, "Mr. Restlin tested it."

The sergeant nodded and stood up. "I'm afraid there aren't going to be any prints in here at all."

Restlin, running a darting finger down the pages of his ledger, looked up. "Why not?"

"It was below freezing last night. The broken glass looks as if a fist was put through it. There are smudged marks on the knob under your prints. The thief undoubtedly wore gloves. Fingerprinting would be a waste of time."

Restlin scrambled around the desk. "Are you trying to say you won't look for the man?"

"No, Mr. Restlin. We'll try to find him for you. We'll see what we can do." He nodded at the ceiling. "Anybody live upstairs here?"

"Yes. There's a family."

"All right. I'll see if they heard or saw anything, and I'll check the house across the street. Meanwhile, if you'll look through your records and see which of your tenants might profit by having your copy of the lease destroyed, we'll talk to them."

"They'll deny it."

"I don't see there's much else we can do, Mr. Restlin."

The little man stormed back to his books. "It's a fine police department, that's all I can say," he threw at Wilks bitterly.

Chief Fellows was taking over at the main desk when Wilks came down the concrete steps to the large basement room in the town hall. The sergeant entered through the side door, bringing in a blast of winter air. "Jesus, it's cold," he said, pulling off his thick leather mittens and the blue wool cap with the ear muffs. He was wearing an army-surplus windbreaker with a wool collar, blue woolen police motorcycle trousers, and black leather boots. "It must be close to zero," he complained. "I don't know what I walked for."

Fellows said, "What was it? A false alarm?"

"No, it was for real." Wilks leaned on the desk to tell him the details. He was a husky man, six feet tall, with wide shoulders and a heavy frame.

Fellows listened in silence. He was a big man too, and older, but some of his weight was in the paunch around his stomach. "That's the damndest thing I ever heard," he said when Wilks was through. He hunched over the desk on his elbows and stared at the steel door to the cell block at the far end of the room. "Now what would anybody want those leases for?"

"To avoid responsibility's the way I see it."

"What kind of responsibility?"

"I'd say somebody wants to renege on a lease some way. If there's no lease, he can't be accused of it."

The chief took a plug of chewing tobacco from his shirt pocket, bit off a piece, and offered it to Wilks, who shook his head. "Now that reminds me of a story," he said, repocketing the tobacco. "There was this hunter who wasn't a very bright guy and when he was coming home empty-handed one evening, he came upon a sign which said '$10 fine for trespassing.' Well, it was late and he was tired, so he cut through the forbidden property anyway and he didn't get far before he had the bad luck to run into the owner. The owner grabbed him and said, 'You're under arrest for trespassing.' So you know what the hunter did? He shot and killed the owner.

"Well, what happened, of course, was he got caught and hung for murder, but that not-so-bright hunter, he died with a smile on his lips. You know why? Because he was thinking to himself: 'I never did get fined that ten dollars.' "

Wilks said, "Get to the point, Fred."

Fellows scratched a cheek. "The point is I don't

think many people are as dumb as that hunter. That's
the intriguing thing about this case. If a guy wants to
run out on a lease, why doesn't he just run? Breaking
and entering is a crime." He chewed thoughtfully.
"Seems to me a fellow'd only do that to hide a worse
crime, not a lesser one."

"You take this seriously then?"

"Yes, I guess I do."

"You want me to fingerprint his office?"

"I don't know, Sid. I don't know about that." He
reached under the counter for the phone book and
hunted up Restlin's number. He got the man on the
phone and said, "What have you found, Mr. Restlin?"

"I'm making a list," Restlin told him. "People who're
behind in their rent. I'm not through yet."

"How many've you got?"

"Five so far."

"Anybody owe much?"

"One family owes two months."

"Well, I'll tell you what you do," Fellows said. "You
hold off doing that and, instead, look up everybody
who's on a short-term lease right now. Then you call
me back."

He hung up, and Wilks said, "You got something on
your mind, Fred?"

"Like I said. Who'd commit a crime to break a
lease?"

Thursday, 11:00—12:00 2

Restlin called back in three quarters of an hour. He was both excited and nervous. "I want to tell you, Chief, I did like you said, and there's one house. There's this guy, name of Campbell, who took the house for a month, signed a month's lease, signed it in January. There's something funny going on around there, because it's available the first of March, and yesterday in the afternoon Watly took a prospect out to look at it and the place was all locked up. There wasn't nobody home."

"Is that unusual on a working day?"

"There wasn't even his wife home. What do you think's the matter? That's one of my own houses. I want to know what's the matter."

The chief said, "I don't know that anything's the matter, Mr. Restlin. That's your only short-term lease?"

"Yes, and he paid in advance. I don't know why you think anything's wrong there. He can't gyp me."

"All the same, Mr. Restlin, suppose we go out and have a look at that house? We'll pick you up." He put down the phone as Wilks came in with two containers of coffee. He said, "Drink up, Sid. We're going to have a look at a house."

"Empty, I suppose."

"It was yesterday afternoon."

"But you don't think it's lease-breaking. You think somebody used it for a hide-out?"

Fellows shrugged. "Hide-out, stolen goods, I don't know. Maybe for nothing."

"Suppose it was a hide-out. Why break in and steal the lease? The guy must've known Restlin would have his name."

Fellows removed the lid of his container and blew on the black coffee inside. "I'm just fumbling around, Sid, that's all. You put sugar in this?"

"No. I remembered."

"Good." He sipped and made a face and said, "I hate coffee without milk and sugar. Go get Unger to take over here, will you? He's in communications."

Wilks and Fellows picked up Restlin about twenty after eleven and the three drove out to the house in the black police station wagon. The two policemen had little to say, but Frank Restlin was voluble. "The fellow paid cash for it. What would he want to steal the lease for? You ought to look at the people who owe me money. You ought to take fingerprints."

The house was out of town nearly three miles, the first one on the left off Old Town Road on Highland. It was a white bungalow with five small rooms, a cellar and an attic, set back fifty feet with a dry, bare lawn around it. There was a drive on the right to an unpainted one-car garage in back and the acre of property on which it stood was mostly woods. The nearest house was a hundred yards away across the street.

Fellows swung the car into the drive and they got out by the garage. There were a couple of clothespoles with an old sagging line, a weather-beaten seesaw, and a broken sandbox leaking its contents by the deeper grass at the edge of the yard. The chief, in a leather jacket, fishing cap, blue riding pants, and laced leather boots, crunched across the hard ground to the back porch. He stamped on the planks and looked at the windows as he rang the bell. The two on the left were shaded and the one on the right stared back emptily. The whole atmosphere was desertion and disuse. "I don't think anybody's home today either," he said. "You might try one of those keys, Mr. Restlin."

Restlin obeyed. He bent and fitted a cold key into a cold lock and twisted. He pushed the door open into a short narrow hall to the kitchen. It took another key to unlock the kitchen door and the vaporous breath of the three men swirled in the small area.

They went in, Restlin first, and he nearly tripped over two woman's suitcases standing just inside. Then he let out an anguished shriek and hurried to the sink beside the stove. "The furnace is out! The pipes! The water!" No water came from the faucet, and Restlin ran to the cellar door beside the kitchen entrance and clattered down the stairs. Fellows and Wilks watched him go, and the chief shook his head. "I'll bet that man's got an ulcer." He paused and sniffed the air like a hound dog getting a scent. "What's that smell?"

It was a faint and slightly unpleasant, but unidentifiable odor, and one that, if he detected it at all, didn't interest Sergeant Wilks. "I don't know," he said, dismissing it in favor of the suitcases. "It doesn't look like they left here for good." He lifted each to determine that they were packed and set them down again. They were relatively new, of different sizes, made of pale green lacquered plastic with the initials J.S. stamped in gold under the handles. "J.S.," he said, "doesn't stand for Campbell." He tested the clasps and found them locked.

Fellows sniffed the air again and said, "Well, we're here. Let's take a look around." He stepped through an open door on the left and found himself in a tiny hall with three other doors. The one on the left revealed a small darkened back bedroom which he looked into and shut off again. The one in front was to the bathroom and the one on the right opened into a still smaller bedroom with a dining room beyond. It was a gray day, and the rooms were cramped, dim, cold, and dingy.

Fellows wandered through into the dining room, less interested in the rooms than in following the scent. Wilks followed, his eyes roving. An open door on the right led into the living room, and Fellows stopped again. "It smells stronger here," he said to Wilks. "What does it remind you of?"

Wilks tried the air himself and shrugged. "Remember the time the guy wanted to sue the exterminator? The rats ate the poison and died in the walls and stank up the place?"

"It's not like that, though."

"Not as strong, maybe."

"Not quite the same kind of smell."

"Well, don't worry about it."

"I want to know what it is."

The house was poorly designed as well as poorly constructed. The dining room and kitchen were at opposite corners, connected through the small bedroom on one side and through an L-shaped living room on the other. The front door of the house opened directly into the living room. The coat closet and dining room doors were to its right, the chimney section and door to the attic stairs directly ahead, while the living room itself extended to the left and around the corner. The fireplace was unfortunately placed, being adjacent to the kitchen, and the furnishings, Restlin's own, did nothing to help matters. A couch was against the windows, facing the fireplace. There was an easy chair beside the kitchen door, an end table and lamp by one arm of the couch, and a small rug on the floor. The front section of the room was almost barren. A small telephone table stood by the attic door, a larger table and lamp was in the center of the area with another easy chair beside. There was a straight chair in the corner and another insufficient rug on the floor. A bare radiator stretched halfway across the two front windows.

Fellows walked slowly through the room and then got down in front of the fireplace. "Something they burned?" he suggested. The ashes were old and gray with some charred bits in them. There was a blackened stub of a small log, but nearly everything else had been completely consumed.

Restlin pulled open the kitchen door suddenly and leaned over the arm of the chair to get to the kneeling chief. "The pipes've burst," he said as if he wanted to cry. "They let the fire go out and they didn't turn off the water. This is one of my houses! It's Watly's fault!"

Fellows didn't look up. "You got water in the cellar?"

"No. It's frozen in the pipes. I shut it off. You got to make them pay for this."

"That's right, Mr. Restlin," the chief said without paying attention. He reached up for a poker that hung from a knob projecting from the bricks and said to Wilks, "This doesn't look like wood ashes to me, Sid. Not all of it." He poked the remains.

Restlin said, "You gotta find him, Chief. Come on. Let's go."

"Go where, Mr. Restlin?" The poker pushed up a blackened piece of metal, and Fellows, pulling off a glove, reached in for it.

Restlin edged closer around the chair. "What's that?"

"A knife, wouldn't you say?" The chief lifted it out by its point. "A carving knife with the handle burned off." He handed it to Wilks and poked again and pulled out a hacksaw, also with the handle burned away. The steel of both items was blackened by heat, but like the ashes and the house itself, they were long cold.

Fellows poked some more, but produced nothing else.

He hung up the poker, got to his feet, and slid his hand back into his glove. "Well, Sid. You might have something about those rats."

Restlin said, "That's all very good, but it isn't going to help find them, you know."

Wilks said, "What does burnt flesh smell like, Fred?"

"Don't know. My wife's too good a cook."

"I was thinking—"

"I know what you're thinking, Sid."

Restlin said, "Why don't you two speak English? What's got into you? They've gone and every minute you waste here they're getting farther away."

Fellows turned to him. "Mr. Restlin, I'd appreciate it if you wouldn't keep trying to tell us our business. We want to look around this place and we'd like to have it quiet. Sid, you'd better leave those things here and we'll see what we can find."

The chief retraced his steps, but this time he was paying attention. He paused to look in the closet by the front door, then re-entered the dining room for a quick look around. It was a neat and tidy room containing a buffet, six chairs around a table, and two more chairs in corners, and gave the impression of little use. He paused only briefly there before returning to the small adjacent bedroom. It was a cramped place with barely room for a double bed and a bureau in the corners against the windows, but it showed signs of usage. The bed was hastily made and wrinkled, the way a man makes a bed, and Fellows started his hunt there. A closet under the attic stairs was bare of everything but half a dozen coat hangers, and the chief moved on to the bureau drawers. They too were empty and looked unused. He pulled back the coverlet from two pillows which showed faint indentations. He peered closely and sniffed, then took off his glove and picked up a long black hair. He laid it carefully on top of its pillow and recovered it with the spread. "What's the name of these people again, Mr. Restlin?"

"Campbell," Restlin said with ill-concealed annoyance at the leisurely manner of the chief.

"Mrs. Campbell a brunette?"

"I don't know. I never saw her. I never saw him for that matter."

Fellows gave him an expression of mild surprise. "You rented the place to him sight unseen?"

"Watly rented it. Watly knows him."

"I see." Fellows went out the opposite door and looked into the bathroom. The bottom of the tub was stained and scummy-looking as if it had been washed out but not scrubbed. He went on to the back bedroom, darkened by drawn shades. The room was barren and gloomy. There was a vacant bureau, a straight chair, two night tables and lamps and a double bed stripped to the mattress with the uncovered pillows lying awry at the top.

Fellows left the others at the door and crossed the room to raise the shade by the bureau. He opened the drawers one by one and found nothing but a white button lying on the paper lining of the middle drawer. He left it there, noted that there were no closets, and came out again. "I don't know, Sid," he said. "It looks pretty clean. If it weren't for those suitcases in the kitchen, I'd think they just packed up and left."

Restlin was edgy now. "What do you think's happened?"

"I can't tell you, Mr. Restlin. I'm not sure at all."

"What's that smell supposed to be? It's all over the house."

Fellows shrugged. "I don't know that either. It might be something they burned in the fireplace, it might be because the house has been shut up tight a couple of days. Did you notice it down in the cellar?"

Restlin said, "I didn't notice anything down in the cellar. I was looking at the pipes. They busted those pipes on me. They let the fire go out and they didn't shut off the water valve. I gotta replace all those pipes."

They went into the kitchen, where the chief stared thoughtfully at the suitcases. Restlin said, "I can't get those pipes fixed right away, and here I got a man wants to rent this place starting the first of March. He wants a year's lease. I'm getting gypped."

"I can't help you on that, Mr. Restlin. I'm not a plumber." Fellows opened the cellar door and went down the steps sniffing his way into the dimness below with Wilks and Restlin following.

There were coalbins at the front and a preserve closet and a woodbin, well-stocked with logs. An old washing machine was near the stairs, the furnace was in the center of the floor, and the rest of the area was vacant except along one side back of the woodbin. An accumulation of items was there, some old and broken furniture, a trunk under a dusty sheet, with rusty ceiling fixtures on top, a stack of bushel baskets, a lawn mower, snow shovel, and gardening tools.

"I don't smell anything down here," Wilks said. "It must be something they burned."

"That's my guess," Fellows said, but he wasn't disposed to let the matter alone. He looked into the bin compartments and preserve closet and came back to the dead furnace. Wilks said, "What're you looking for now? They've moved out."

"They moved out several days ago, but they left two suitcases." The chief opened the furnace door and peered in at the dead ashes, started to close it again, but stopped for another look. "Sid, come here."

Wilks bent over the chief's shoulder for a view. "I see ashes."

"Coal ashes?"

"Those aren't coal ashes. Not on top. I don't know what they are."

Fellows closed the grate door gently. "Mr. Restlin, you rent this place furnished?"

"Yes, yes, of course. Watly turned it over to the guy

for a month, complete with everything, linen, silver, coal, electricity, local phone service, everything."

"All this stuff along the wall is yours?"

"Certainly. Of course."

"That trunk?"

Restlin wasn't sure. "If it isn't mine, I'm going to keep it anyway to pay for the pipes. The suitcases and the trunk and everything in them."

Fellows pulled up the corner of the dusty sheet. Then he removed the fixtures and uncovered the trunk. It was a solidly constructed metal affair painted green and decorated with two initials in faded yellow. The initials were the same as on the suitcases, J.S.

"The only thing missing are the people," Fellows said. He tested the lock and it didn't open. He tried to move the trunk, and it didn't budge. He bent close and sniffed at the edges of the lid, then took off his glove and tried the lock once more. He said very soberly, "Sid, go out to the car and get a screwdriver. Let's see if we can't force this thing."

Wilks started to say, "They might come back for it—" But something about the chief's voice stopped him. He went up the stairs.

The screwdriver was large and strong, but so was the lock. Wilks's first efforts only dented the metal of the trunk. He kept prying until he worked the wedge of steel well under the clasp. This time, when he bore on it, the lock popped.

Restlin wet his lips. It was another case of breaking and entering, and he started to mention it, but Fellows and Wilks were busy unhooking the side clasps. They threw back the lid and revealed crammed wads of feminine attire, two overcoats, jackets, stadium boots, spring dresses. It was the sort of thing one would expect to find in any woman's trunk, except the winter clothes were mixed with the summer and the smell of mothballs was mixed with a fainter and less pleasant odor.

They didn't speak but pitched in. Wilks lifted out an armload of clothes and Fellows spread the sheet for him to put them on. They removed a tray and went after the things underneath. Restlin peered over their shoulder and said, "What's that funny smell?"

Fellows nudged him aside when he lifted out dresses wadded as no woman ever packed dresses. "Please keep back, Mr. Restlin."

Restlin didn't stay back. He went around beside Wilks and tried to get a look. When the sergeant reached the end of the clothes on his side, Restlin peered closer at what lay beneath. "What's that?" he said.

Fellows's next armload revealed the rest of the answer, and Restlin shrieked. He said, "Oh my God," and ran across the cellar up the stairs.

Dr. James MacFarlane, the Stockford medical examiner, trudged slowly up the cellar steps with his little black bag in his hand. In the kitchen, two ambulance attendants were sitting in their overcoats at the table in the breakfast nook, smoking a cigarette and having a cup of black coffee. They gestured at the living room when he asked for the chief and he went on through, past a policeman who was shoveling the fireplace ashes into a paper bag, toward the chief, who was standing near the front door talking with two reporters.

"It was a body," Fellows was saying. "White, female, dark hair. That's all we know."

"Was she pretty?"

"It's a truncated torso. Head, arms, and most of the legs cut off." He turned when MacFarlane came up. "Well, Jim, anything you can add?"

The medical examiner shook his head. "She's been dead anywhere from three days to a week or even longer. May be pretty hard to determine what the cause of death was. You photographed her yet?"

"Hank Lemmon of the *Bulletin* took some pictures for me before you got here. You ready to take her away?"

"Yeah. You going to want that sheet spread out in front of the trunk with the clothes on it?"

"You can use it, only don't get those clothes dirty."

The doctor nodded. "I'll work on her over at the hospital. By the way, it looks as if some of the abdominal organs have been removed."

"Any skill involved?"

"None whatever. Whoever did it knows nothing about anatomy—not so much as a butcher."

"And she's been dead at least three days?"

"Probably much longer. She was dead some time before the attempt to dismember her."

Wilks came down the stairs from the attic. "Nothing up there, Fred. Nothing at all."

"Set a couple of the boys to work fingerprinting the house. I want every room."

Wilks went off and MacFarlane went with him. The policeman who'd been cleaning out the fireplace came up with the bag of its contents. The chief said, "That goes to the State Police lab, Henderson. You got it marked?"

"Yes, sir."

"O.K. Now you get another bag and go down in the basement and collect all the ashes in the furnace. They go to the lab too."

One of the reporters said, "How did you come to find her?"

"The missing leases I told you about. I guessed the only reason for stealing them was to remove a handwriting specimen. People don't do that for nothing."

"And the man's name is John Campbell?"

"That's what Restlin says. Now I can't tell you any more, so if you'll kind of wait outside, so you don't track anything around in here, I'll be much obliged." He ushered them out the front door, down the stone slab in front to the cold dry grass. A screen of trees blocked the view of Old Town Road. The woods on the other side of the drive were dense. Across Highland Road in front were woods, but a hundred yards down, stood a clean white house. One of the reporters pulled out a cigarette, and Fellows said, "I'd appreciate it if you wouldn't smoke around here, mister. I've got five men out back combing the yard and I wouldn't want them coming around and bringing in one of your butts for a clue. Might confuse us some."

He left them there and walked down between the ambulance and six cars that filled the drive and lined the road, starting for the house across the way. Midway there, he turned once for a look back at the murder bungalow. It was white, small, unprepossessing and isolated, all features that made it ideal for the purpose. The reporters had got back in their car, probably to smoke and keep warm, and the front yard was deserted. The men in the back were hidden by the cars in the drive and no one was in evidence just then. Fellows turned and continued to the larger white house across the way. A white curtain fell in place behind a first-floor window there and when he got to the porch, a woman opened the door the moment he rang the bell. She was fiftyish, gray and stout, and she wore glasses. Her name, according to the mailbox by the walk, was Banks and she said an expectant, "Yes?"

Fellows introduced himself with his hat properly in his hand and was invited into the parlor. "What's happening, Inspector?" the woman asked, hardly withholding her curiosity until she closed the door. "All those cars—all those policemen."

"Little trouble with those what's-their-names," Fellows said, standing until the woman took a seat in a high-backed rocker so placed that she could look through the window curtains up the road. He sat then, near the window.

"The Campbells?" She rocked contentedly. "I'm not surprised."

"Know anything about them?"

"Not much," Mrs. Banks said primly. "Not very sociable, and I mind my own business."

"Ever seen them, Mrs. Banks?"

"Oh, yes indeed. Mr. Banks and I went to call on them a couple of Sundays back. Not very welcoming, I will say. She dresses fancy, but there was dust in the corners. She gave us tea. Tried to offer us liquor. That kind of woman." She rocked a little more vigorously in disapproval.

"What'd she look like?"

"Brunette. Wore lipstick. That kind of woman."

"There're quite a few women of that kind, Mrs. Banks. That doesn't exactly identify her."

"Well, I suppose there are those who would call her pretty."

"About how old was she?"

"Youngish, but old enough to know better. Not very well brought up, I will say."

"You called on her just once?"

"Mr. Banks and me. We wanted to be neighborly. It's the decent thing to do, Inspector. Can't say it was a pleasure. She wasn't very welcoming and she never returned the call. Had her hair in curlers when we arrived. Sunday afternoon, too. She had a blue and white bandana around her head and a house dress, light blue with tiny white figures. But she had her lipstick on. We dressed up. Mr. Banks and I wouldn't go around like that on a Sunday, especially when neighbors drop in, but she didn't seem to care. Not that one. She could have put her hands on the liquor soon enough, but she had trouble finding tea."

"What was Mr. Campbell like?"

"He warn't there. He was off on a business trip, so she said. Never did see the man."

"You see Mrs. Campbell any other time?"

"Saw her just about any time she left the house, but

it wasn't much. She'd come out once in a while to hang up some clothes in her back yard. You can see the yard from here except for those cars in the drive. I guess her husband must've done the shopping; well, she called him her husband, but I noticed she didn't wear any wedding ring. 'Tany rate, she didn't have a car and there's no place you can go around here without a car. I know because I don't drive. That's why we women along this road are right neighborly and I was being generous because it can be pretty lonesome out here if you don't have any neighbors to kind of chin with on the phone or walk over to visit, but she was the lonesome kind, I guess. Leastwise, she didn't make no effort to be friendly."

Fellows rubbed his chin and was about to ask more questions about the mysterious Mr. Campbell when Mrs. Banks got half out of her chair. "Say, now, what's that?"

Fellows, nearer the window, turned his chair and pulled aside the curtain. The two ambulance men were coming into view from behind the cars, carrying the sheet-wrapped torso on a stretcher. It looked like a lump of bedding riding in the middle of the taut canvas. Seen anywhere else, it would never suggest a body and even on a stretcher one wouldn't suspect it was the body of an adult.

Mrs. Banks hurried to the window to watch the procession, the stretcher followed by Dr. MacFarlane and two policemen. "Why," she cried. "It's a child. They've killed a child. Why that's an ambulance. I thought it was the police wagon."

"There's been an accident," Fellows said, rising in courtesy.

"They're kidnappers, aren't they?" she said, her eyes glued to the window.

"We're not sure what they are, Mrs. Banks." The chief shifted his feet. He knew further questioning would be fruitless while there was something to watch, so he waited patiently until the doors of the ambulance were closed and it backed around in the road, turned left at the corner, and disappeared from sight.

"Well, I never," Mrs. Banks said, coming away. "Well, I never."

She went back to her seat, and the chief took his own again. "We were talking about Mr. Campbell."

"Yes, well he had the car and he was away all day. He must have left real early in the morning and he was never around week-ends. He'd get home around half past five most of the time, but then he'd drive right off again. Then he'd come back around eight and he'd be there for a couple of hours and then sometimes he'd go off again, 'long about half past ten and once, when we were in bed, he drove out about eleven. When he came back after that, or if he came back at all, I never knew, but I do know his car was never around when we got up in the morning."

"Which is what time?"

"Half past six."

"And he was away every weekend?"

"Never saw hide nor hair of him weekends. Business trip his wife said. Monkey business, I say."

"I don't suppose you'd know what kind of a car it was?"

"No. He always got home after dark. He was never around when it was light." She hesitated. "Wait a minute. There was one afternoon when he came home. That was a strange one."

"What happened, Mrs. Banks?"

"It was about three o'clock in the afternoon. I was cleaning around upstairs when I saw this car pull up. Ford car, it was, tan, pretty new. Well, Inspector, out gets Mr. Campbell, big as life, and he's got a vacuum cleaner in his hand, you know, one of those long round things on a slide? He was wearing a brown hat and a tan overcoat and he went up to the door, and Mrs.

Campbell let him in. Well, they were in there for about
twenty minutes and suddenly he and she come to the
front door again and he doesn't have his coat or hat on
and he's in his shirt sleeves. He closes the door and
jumps back into the car and drives into the drive.
Then, when he was coming around to the front of the
house, the grocer boy drove up. That was the only time
I ever saw the grocer make a delivery there. He had a
bag of groceries and Mr. Campbell took it and paid for
it and then he went back inside. He was in there for at
least an hour and a half, because I saw the car there
that long and then, a few minutes later, I saw that his
car was gone. That was around four-thirty or quarter
of five, Inspector, and then he came back at five-thirty,
because my husband was home and I was telling him
about it when I saw the lights of Mr. Campbell's car
and this time he went right into the drive and in the
house and he didn't go right out again like he usually
did. This time he was there all evening until after we
went to bed, but he was gone again the next morning."

Fellows had his notebook out and was jotting down
the pertinent items. He looked up. "You remember exactly what day that was?"

"Friday the thirteenth."

"What did Mr. Campbell look like?"

"He was pretty far away, Inspector, and my eyesight
isn't what it used to be. Tall, I would call him, but I
couldn't say more than that." She leaned forward.
"He's done something terrible, hasn't he?"

"We think he hasn't been behaving himself very well.
What color hair did he have? You saw him without a
hat."

"Oh, dark hair. Tall and dark and slender. I couldn't
tell anything about his face."

Fellows nodded and made notations. "Now, Mrs.
Banks, can you tell me the last time you saw Mrs.
Campbell?"

Mrs. Banks hesitated. "Well, I can't say. I'd judge a

week or more ago." She covered the lapse by saying,
"Of course I'm not nosey and I don't pry and she might
have been around a lot when I wasn't looking."

"But at least a week ago is the last time?"

"Far's I remember."

"Did you recognize the grocery boy? Do you know
what store he delivers for?"

"Oh my, no. I don't know anything about those delivery boys. My husband takes me shopping." She
peered past his shoulder. "My, look at all the cars.
They're blocking the whole road."

Chief Fellows turned and saw. The word had been
spread and now a horde of sight-seers was descending
on the quiet of Highland Road. He thanked the woman
and took a hasty leave.

Fellows went back to the murder house and ordered the sight-seers who were congregating in the front yard back into their cars. "Move on. There's nothing to see. Keep moving." Then he went inside and ordered two policemen to chase away the cars of anybody not authorized to be there and to set up a road block at the corner. "I don't want anybody coming down this road who doesn't have business here." After that, he hunted up Wilks, who was busy fingerprinting the house.

"It's useless," the detective sergeant told him. "Looks like the guy wiped everything with a towel, door frames, doors, everything. The best we've got are a couple of smudges that aren't any good."

"You inventorying the place?"

"As we go along."

"Got anybody you can spare?"

"They're all busy, why?"

"We're going to have to do some checking of grocery stores. Well, we can let that go until I come back. I want to get down to the real estate office."

Wilks said, "Give Restlin my love."

Frank Restlin, however, was not at the office. "He went home," Watly explained. "He was feeling sick. It was really a murder?"

"There was a body. We don't know yet how she died." Fellows pulled off his gloves and cap and un-zipped his jacket. "Restlin was telling me you're the one who handled the rent. You want to tell me about it?"

Watly wet his lips. He got out cigarettes and offered one to Fellows, who shook his head and resorted to his chewing tobacco instead. "I wish I hadn't handled it now, believe me," the real estate agent said. "Mr. Rest-lin blames me for what happened—the pipes freezing, especially. He's feeling pretty bad about that."

"Worse than about the body, I'll bet."

Watly smiled, but not happily. "You probably aren't kidding. He'd take it out of my pay, I'll bet, if he thought I could afford it, but certainly, I couldn't see anything wrong with the man."

Fellows sat down in a chair by the desk and fumbled for his notebook. "Tell me the whole story now, clear as you can remember, dates and times and what was said and any peculiarities the man might have had, any-thing you can remember about his looks and manner."

Watly, taking Restlin's seat behind the desk, pulled his lip and dragged on the cigarette. "It was an after-noon. Twenty-third of January. I can tell you that be-cause when Mr. Restlin came back all pale and white and told me what you found, I immediately looked up Campbell's application. That was the day he came in, the twenty-third of January around the middle of the afternoon. Mr. Restlin was out with a prospect showing him some properties. This fellow Campbell came in. He was in his thirties, I'd guess, maybe thirty-seven or -eight, and he had dark hair, a moderate build, and stood about two inches shorter than me. He was about five-ten, I'd say. He told me he was interested—"

"What about his clothes?"

"Clothes?" Watly thought about that. "No hat. A tan overcoat with a plaid scarf. Red plaid. Dark trou-sers as I recall—he didn't take off his coat—and-uhbrown shoes, well shined. They looked like pretty nice clothes. Better clothes than I could afford."

"Go on."

"He said he was only going to be in town a short time and he wanted a house for a month. He said he wanted it completely furnished. He was a company representative or something like that. A salesman, I gathered, or some job where he moved around a lot. At least that's the impression he gave.

"I said we had something he might like, two or three things, in fact, and he wanted the cheapest we could give him. I said the house on Highland Road was the cheapest, but it was pretty isolated. That didn't seem to bother him at all. He seemed to prefer it that way. I told him he could have it for a hundred dollars for the month of February and that would include everything. I did try to interest him in one of the other houses because, well, they cost a little more and he looked like he could afford it. He looked used to nice things and this house isn't the best we've got."

"Did he say anything about a Mrs. Campbell?"

"He did say he'd need an extra key for his wife. That's about the only time I remember him mentioning her, but I certainly got the impression he was married."

"Did you show him the house?"

"I did. I drove him out. It'd been vacant since October and I offered to take him through it, but all he did was look at it from the outside as we drove by and that satisfied him. He didn't bother to have me stop and, in fact, he seemed to go out to look at it with me more because he was supposed to than because he cared. I don't know if that's important or not, Chief."

"Everything's important, Mr. Watly. Then what?"

"I drove him back here and he signed the lease and paid the money. He had it on him."

"What about references?"

Watly said, "Oh, he had them. They're on his application." He got up and went to the file cabinet, sorted quickly through the contents of the drawer above the one that had been robbed, and came back with it. He sat down and pressed his fingertips together on the desk while the chief studied it. "Employed by Gary Hardware Company, Erie, Pennsylvania," Fellows said, and looked up. "I don't see any character references listed."

"He said anyone at Gary from the president on down would be glad to vouch for him."

"You check on this?"

"Mr. Restlin didn't bother. It's a reputable firm."

"No last address?"

"He said he's usually in hotels. He moved around a lot. This time I got the impression he and his wife wanted to try housekeeping for a change."

Fellows laid the paper on the desk. "This application isn't very well filled out."

"I guess that's my fault."

"He didn't sign it either. This his writing?"

Watly looked most uncomfortable. "It's mine. I filled it out." He went on to explain. "Mr. Campbell was in a hurry. He grabbed the first house he looked at. In fact, he hardly cared to go out and see it. He wanted to sign the lease right away and he had the money out as soon as we got back. That house isn't too easy to rent, and I knew Mr. Restlin wouldn't want to lose out on it, so I couldn't be too fussy. Mr. Campbell chafed at the idea of an application since the house was available, so I hurriedly asked him a few questions just as a matter of form and I wrote down the answers myself. It wasn't like he was taking it for a longer period and would be paying rent. Then we'd check very carefully on his ability to pay. But this was in advance and he certainly looked reputable. His firm is, and I know that because I did look that up. We didn't check any further, though. Mr. Restlin and I didn't think it was necessary."

"I'm afraid that was a mistake, Mr. Watly."

"I guess it was, but we didn't dream—"

"All right, no matter. I have the idea he planned it that way. I think you were being used, so it's not your fault." Fellows shifted his tobacco to the other cheek. "Ever see him again?"

"No, sir. I gave him the keys and said we'd have the water turned on and the heat up by the time he was ready to take over. I did that myself on the last day of January. Neither Mr. Restlin nor I have been back since."

"You have no samples whatever of Campbell's handwriting?"

Watly shook his head. "Only his signature on the lease, and that's gone."

"And that," said Fellows, getting to his feet, "is probably the reason it's gone."

The chief, when he left the real estate office, drove back out to the scene of the crime. He stopped at the corner to send the shivering traffic officer off for some late lunch, then parked in front of the house where a total of eight other cars now stood. Four reporters on the front lawn converged on him when he got out. "We've been looking for you, Chief. They told us at headquarters you were out here."

"No new developments," Fellows said. "We're right where we were."

They trooped along with him toward the house. "The husband do it?"

"If it's murder and he was her husband, then the husband probably did it."

"He might not be her husband?"

"We don't know who he was yet." The chief opened the front door and saw one of the officers inside. "Hey, Lawlor. Have you searched the front yard?"

"All done, Chief. Didn't find anything."

"O.K. Get to the corner and handle traffic will you? Smitty, if you're done, take an hour for some lunch and get back here. Take the rest of the men with you except those who're working." He went into the kitchen and found Wilks. The sergeant said, "I heard you. Nobody's working."

"All finished?"

"Finished with fingerprints. There aren't any. Finished with the inventory, except for what's in the suitcases. We're brewing a pot of Campbell's coffee. You want some?"

"What a lazy bum." Fellows sat down at the kitchen table. Two other officers were in the room. One of them took the pot off the stove and started pouring.

"Not much food in the house," Wilks said. "Just coffee and a few cans of things. They must have lived pretty much day to day."

"That reminds me. As soon as everybody gets back from lunch, start them on a canvass of all grocery stores that deliver. A delivery was made here Friday the thirteenth. Campbell paid for it in person."

Wilks made a note of it, and Fellows said, "By the way, that inventory of yours include vacuum cleaners?"

Wilks waved at the kitchen closet beside the stove. "An old one in there. Prewar."

Fellows got up to look at it. It was a Eureka with a cloth bag and a long handle. He unwound the cord, plugged it into a socket, and tested the switch. The motor came on purring evenly and the bag filled with air. He switched it off, unplugged it, and put it away again.

Wilks said, "What's that for?"

"Just wondering what they might need another vacuum cleaner for." He accepted a cup of the coffee. "Any others around?"

"No. There supposed to be?"

Fellows brought the coffee to the table. "The woman down the road saw the guy bring a new one in one day. She didn't see it leave."

Wilks grinned. "Is that supposed to mean it's still here?"

"She doesn't miss much. Of course Campbell could have taken it away again at night. I think she might not quite see it from her window in the dark."

"Real eager, huh?"

"I think she's a British mystery-story fan. Kept calling me 'Inspector.' Any milk for this coffee?"

"There's milk in the icebox, but it's sour."

"Well, it's better if I drink it black anyway, I suppose." He sipped the steaming dark liquid. "Henderson get the ashes out of the furnace?"

"He's on his way to Hartford with them now."

"Well, we'll drink this and leave a couple of men here and go in for some lunch. I didn't eat any breakfast and this stuff isn't nourishing. And I want to get in touch with the Erie police."

"What for?"

"To check on Campbell. He listed himself on his application as working for the Gary Hardware Company there. I don't suppose he does, but I want to make sure."

"What else did you find?"

"The girl didn't wear a wedding ring. And I got a description of Campbell. Tall, dark, medium build, tan overcoat. No hat when Watly saw him, but he wore a brown one when the woman across the way got a look."

"And he brought in a vacuum cleaner? What the hell for?"

Fellows shrugged. "It beats me."

Thursday, 5
3:30—5:30 P.M.

042   FILE 2   PD STOCKFORD CT   FEB 26—59
PD ERIE PENNA

REQUEST INFO JOHN CAMPBELL DARK HAIR 5—10 WT
160 AGE 30—40 EMPLOYED GARY HARDWARE CO UR
CITY WANTED ON SUSPICION OF MURDER PLEASE CON-
FIRM

AUTH   F C FELLOWS   OPR NORTON 3—30 PM
ZZZZZ

ZZZZZ

ALARM 321 CODE SIG 12   AUTH F C FELLOWS
FEB 26—59 ARREST FOR MURDER JOHN CAMPBELL
WHITE 35—5—10—160 SLIM DARK HAIR DRIVES TAN
LATE MODEL FORD

OPR NORTON 3—48 PM

064   FILE 8   PD ERIE PENNA   FEB 26—59
PD STOCKFORD CT

CAMPBELL VICE PRES GARY HARDWARE CO AGE 53 HT
5—9 WT 165 HAIR GRAY REQUEST INSTRUCTIONS

AUTH   T F PRENDERGAST   OPR RIKERS 4—29 PM
ZZZZZ

042   FILE 2   PD STOCKFORD CT   FEB 26—59
PD ERIE PENNA

INVESTIGATE WHEREABOUTS JOHN CAMPBELL FEB 1—
26 AGE AND HAIR WRONG CAN YOU SEND PHOTO
CAMPBELL

AUTH F C FELLOWS   OPR NORTON 4—47 PM
ZZZZZ

064   FILE 8   PD ERIE PENNA   FEB 26—59

PD STOCKFORD CT
CAMPBELL IN NASSAU JAN 23—FEB 23 RETURNED
TO WORK FEB 24 CONFIRM HAIR GRAY AGE 53 ONLY
JOHN CAMPBELL IN GARY HARDWARE RECORDS SEND-
ING PHOTO

AUTH T C PRENDERGAST   OPR RIKERS 5—19 PM
ZZZZ

Chief Fellows was looking over the shoulder of the
girl in communications when the last message came in.
He tore off the sheet and scowled at it. "Tell them to
hold up—no. Tell them I want that alibi checked out,
Doris." He took the paper with him back to the headquarters room downstairs.

Sergeant William S. Gorman was on the desk and
three reporters were talking with him, with Sergeant
Wilks, and plainclothesman Edward I. Lewis. Fellows
said, "I guess you can all see this," and passed the message to Wilks, who read it and handed it around.

Wilks said, "I don't suppose Watly's eyesight could
be so bad he'd call a fifty-three-year-old man in his
thirties, even with dyed hair."

Gorman, who had come on at four and been catching up on events ever since, said, "That time element, though. Campbell left for Nassau on the twenty-third of January and that was the day Campbell rented the house."

One of the reporters said, "What about it, Chief?"

Fellows smiled. "Now wouldn't I be a fool to go speculate in front of the press?"

"Is there a chance it's the same guy?"

"The Erie police are going to check his alibi. I'll tell you when we get the reports and when we show Watly his picture."

"If it's not the right Campbell, would that mean someone's trying to impersonate him?"

"Your guess is as good as mine."

"What's the next move?"

"Sergeant Wilks and I are going out to look over the house again."

Wilks said, "Hey, I've been all over it, Fred. It's been checked thoroughly."

"Not by me." He smiled. "Come on, Sid, what do you want to do, go home early?"

"It's not going to be the same Campbell," Wilks said to Fellows as they drove out to the house in the gathering darkness. "No man in his right mind would use his real name renting a house to kill someone in."

"I'll go along with that, Sid, but it's interesting that there really is a Campbell at the Gary Hardware plant. Our Mr. Campbell told Watly everybody from the president on down would vouch for him. Sounds like he had the vice president in mind."

"I'll guess that's an angle we'd better follow. It's probably someone who knows the real Campbell, probably someone who worked at Gary at one time."

"And," Fellows added, "the woman wouldn't be his wife. A wife would object to using an assumed name. Probably one or both of them were married to someone else too."

"Why married, necessarily?"

"Same reason. Assumed name."

"And he probably meant to kill her all along. It's a nice love-nest setup and he could sell it to her for that, but it's even better for a murder. She's been dead quite a spell already and nobody would still suspect anything if he hadn't stolen the leases."

"That's the one thing I wonder about," Fellows said. "Cutting up the body was obviously for purposes of disposal. Why did he steal the lease before he finished getting rid of it?" He added slowly, "Cold feet?"

"Cold house."

"Or a weak stomach?" Fellows turned the corner onto Highland Road and pulled up behind a lone car parked in front of the house.

"Whose is that?" Wilks wondered.

They found the answer up on the lawn where patrolman Manny was keeping the house under surveillance. With him was a young man in his early thirties, wearing a brown coat and hat with a press card in the band. The man held out a hand as the chief came up and said, "I'm Hilders of the Bridgeport *Courier*. I've been assigned to the case."

Fellows said, "That's a coincidence. I've been assigned to it too."

"You going inside now?"

"That's right. The sergeant and me—only."

"Give a guy a break."

"If we find anything, we'll let you know, Mr. Hilders. But I wouldn't suggest waiting out here in the cold. I'll be making my statements at headquarters."

"And if you don't mind, Chief, I'll be making my investigation on *my* own."

"O.K. You find something, you can let us know." He said to the patrolman, "Any trouble out here?"

"No, sir. Just one car of sight-seers about an hour ago. I didn't let them get out."

"All right. Your relief will be out any minute." Fellows went on to the stoop with Wilks and fitted the key Restlin had turned over to him into the lock. He closed the door behind him, shutting out the reporter, snapped on the lights in the frigid and forbidding living room, and went through the rest of the house, turning on lights in all the rooms. He ended in the kitchen where he turned slowly around. "Pretty bare," he said. "Our friend was kind of careful about clues."

"He was," Wilks said. "No papers in the wastebaskets, no writing, no fingerprints, no nothing that I could see."

"Except a hair on the pillow in one bedroom and a button in a dresser drawer. We'll have to see if that button fits any of the clothes in those suitcases there."

"You want to break them open, Fred?"

Fellows looked down at the suitcases and shook his head. "Kind of nice merchandise to bust. We'll let a locksmith do it in the morning."

They started an examination of the house then. Fellows went to the rear bedroom and looked in at the stripped mattress. Two of the three windows still had their shades down. "This is the larger bedroom," he said. "Two-view exposure and three windows. The other bedroom has two windows and one view. The button was in the drawer here, but the hair was in the other bedroom. They obviously slept there, but if the button fits any of the woman's clothes, she must have had them here. Now why would they sleep in the worse room?"

"If he's married and went back to his wife at night, one room could be for love and the other for sleeping."

"Now, Sid, do you think that makes sense?"

"It makes as much sense as the question. What's the answer got to do with finding Campbell?"

"If we can find the answers to enough questions, we'll turn him up."

"That's not the kind of question I'd ask."

Fellows turned. "All right, Sid, what questions have you got?"

"I'd ask why was the bed stripped? Why are the shades down? And I'd answer by saying that if the house was completely furnished, including linen, and the sheets aren't in the place, he did something with them."

"You didn't find the sheets?"

"They aren't here, Fred. What linen there is is on a shelf in the kitchen closet and they're clean. My guess is she was probably killed here or hidden here and he got rid of the sheets to hide the fact he had a body rotting on them for a week."

"O.K., I'll go along. Next question?"

"What did he do with the missing parts of the body? The only shovel in the house is a snow shovel. There're no signs of digging on the property and the ground's like a rock anyway. There's no new-laid concrete in the cellar. That, plus the burned saw and knife means to me he burned those parts."

Fellows laughed. "I guess that's a fair deduction all right."

"Those are the kind of questions that lead us somewhere, Fred. What difference does it make where they slept?"

"I don't know, Sid. I just ask them to satisfy myself, I guess. For instance, I'd kind of like to know where he burned the head, arms, and legs."

"The furnace, of course. And maybe the fireplace. We'll know when the lab analyzes the ashes."

"But if the fireplace, why, Sid? You try it there and you'll smell up the neighborhood."

"Which may be why the guy got panicked and didn't finish the job."

Fellows clapped him on the shoulder. "You're quite a detective, Sid. I'd promote you except that'd put me out of a job and I'm not aiming to retire for quite a spell."

"What you mean is you get the same answers."

"I've got to go along with you. My only problem is the whys."

"The girl was pregnant. I can answer that one."

Fellows edged past him in the tiny hall and looked into the bathroom. "You're making an assumption there, Sid. The doc hasn't said that yet."

"Why else were some of her organs removed other than to hide the fact?"

The chief shrugged. "Removing organs doesn't hide it, Sid, it points to it." He got down on one knee beside the tub and studied its scummy appearance. "What's your detective ability tell you about this? You think maybe he sawed her up in here?"

"That's where I'd do it and there's no blood anywhere. It would have to be here."

"Seems so. But I'm pretty damned ignorant. For instance, if you wait four or five days before you cut up a body, will there be any bleeding or will the blood be all caked?"

"That's something to ask MacFarlane."

Fellows moved on into the smaller bedroom, the room where the shades were up. He'd had the foresight this time to bring some envelopes and he took one from his shirt pocket as he gently pulled back the bedspread, uncovering the indented pillows. The hair was where he had left it and he carefully placed it in the envelope. He licked the flap, glued it in place, and wrote an identification of the contents on the front.

After tucking the envelope back in his pocket, he got down on his knees and peered beneath the bed and bureau. "Mrs. Banks told me there was dirt in the corners," he said, getting up, "but there's a lot more under the bed. I'm going to want the dust from all of these rooms, each room separate, and we'll send that along to the lab. Better empty that vacuum cleaner too." He made a face. "I hate working with dust, but that's about all the guy's left us."

He moved into the dining room and looked in all the corners and under the furniture, then opened the drawers in the buffet. The top left-hand one contained knives, forks, and spoons. There was table linen in the bottom large drawer. The others were empty. "You fingerprint the silver?"

"No."

"He might've forgotten to wipe that, Sid."

"All right. First thing tomorrow."

In the living room, Fellows stopped by the telephone table. A blank pad stood beside the phone, and the chief regarded it thoughtfully. Wilks said, "We did the phone. It'd been wiped."

"Something was written on the sheet above this blank sheet. There're faint indentations on it."

"Nothing legible. I looked."

"Not yet, anyway." Fellows opened the door to the attic stairs beside the tiny table, found the wall switch, and climbed the steps slowly. Wilks stayed behind and waited while the chief had a look around and came down again shaking his head. "A year's growth of dust on the floors. They never went up there."

"Don't you trust me, Fred? I looked up there this morning."

"I trust you, Sid, I'm just not the executive type. I have to try everything myself." He led the way past the fireplace, swept clean of ashes, and he paused to look at the knife and saw still lying on the hearth where Wilks had left them. They passed into the kitchen again, having made a complete circuit and then they went down to the cellar.

The sheet that had covered the trunk and upon which the clothes had been laid was gone and the clothes themselves were neatly piled on top of the old washing machine. The trunk stood bare and open, dragged from its spot near the wall onto the bare floor by the furnace. Fellows looked it over carefully without touching it. The lid lay back and there was nothing inside it except grains of powder in the crevices. "The woman's trunk and the woman's suitcases, but nothing that belongs to the man." He lifted the lid and let it fall shut, then bent and studied the old yellow initials that adorned it.

"Tell you anything, Fred?"

"Not much. The trunk belongs to the dead girl and she wasn't married. I have to guess the man was."

"How do you know she wasn't married?"

"Stands to reason. These are old initials. The suit-case initials are new and they're the same. No, Sid, the girl was single and the man was married. I'd put a fair-size wager on that."

"Not with me you won't."

Fellows stared down at the trunk in the dim light of the naked bulb by the furnace. "But who is she and where does she come from? That's the question." Then, as if an idea had struck him, he lifted the trunk by one handle and turned it over. There, on the bottom, was a brand-new express label on which was printed in ink, "Mrs. John Campbell, 2 Highland Road, Stockford, Conn."

Wilks said, "Hey, boy," and Fellows said, "Just happened to remember nobody looked at the bottom when the body was in it. Well, the trunk was shipped. That makes it easier."

Wilks said, "I'll check the stationmaster first thing in the morning. If we can find out who the girl is, it shouldn't be hard to find the man."

"You find out what date the trunk was shipped too, Sid. And see if anybody remembers it. I don't guess our station would handle too many trunks."

They left the trunk on its back and climbed the stairs again. Wilks said, "Anything else, Fred?"

Fellows nodded. He went through the living room to the telephone table and paused again at the pad. The indentations weren't legible, but he tore the blank sheet off all the same and held it to the light. "Your inventory turn up any candles in this house, Sid?"

"Five stubs in a drawer in the kitchen. I know this place better than my own home."

"How about iodine?"

"Medicine cabinet in the bathroom."

"Get a candle and the largest spoon you can find, Sid." Fellows went for the iodine and brought it to the kitchen where Wilks was lighting a candle stub and sticking it to a plate. He had laid out a big cooking spoon and Fellows carefully poured the bottle's contents into it. "Now if you'll heat this over the candle, Sid. Not accepted laboratory technique, but we might get some results."

Wilks held the spoon over the flame and when the iodine began to warm, Fellows held the blank sheet of paper above it. He moved it back and forth over the purplish vapors for three or four minutes until it was thoroughly permeated and then laid it aside to cool. Wilks put the spoon down and watched with interest. "Where'd you get this trick, Fred?"

"Criminology books."

As they watched, the paper slowly took on a faintly bluish cast and as the cooling progressed, the indentations turned a slightly darker blue. When the process was complete, the writing was clearly legible. It was in a feminine hand and said, "Jean Sherman, 402 Westville Street, Bridgeport, Connecticut."

"Voilà," said Fellows. "The missing girl."

"Nice of her to leave her name and address."

"Right nice." The chief folded the paper carefully and tucked it in the bulging wallet he took from his hip pocket.

Wilks said, "I wonder if she knew what was going to happen to her."

"I don't think she'd wait. More to the point, though, is what actually did happen." The chief went to the phone and called Dr. MacFarlane.

The doctor didn't have much to report. "This isn't easy," he said. "I can't tell you how she died yet. Some of the vital organs are missing, so I can't rule out poison. It could be a blow on the head or strangulation, but I can't tell that without seeing her head and neck."

"Was she pregnant, Jim?"

"No. That much I have been able to make sure of. The girl wasn't pregnant."

"When did she die?"

MacFarlane was hard put. "I can't pin that down too closely yet. She'd been in that trunk in below-freezing temperatures for some time and parts of the body were frozen. I'd say at least four days and no more than eight."

"Probably last weekend sometime?"

"Between Wednesday and Sunday. I don't want to say any more than that. I should be able to cut it closer tomorrow."

When Fellows hung up, he and Wilks turned out the lights, locked up the house again, and left, taking with them the two green initialed suitcases. A new policeman was on watch, pacing and stamping in the bitter cold. He had the six-to-eight shift, for Fellows was changing the lonely guard duty every two hours. The patrolman had seen no one and the reporter's car was gone.

The two detectives drove back to headquarters, and Fellows briefed the sergeant on the next day's activities. "Get these suitcases open, Sid, and inventory their contents. And when that picture of Campbell comes in, show it to Watly. I'm sure it's not the same Campbell, we wouldn't be that lucky, but we've got to make it official."

"And I'll keep the men on the grocery-store detail."

"Yeah. I want the boy who made the delivery. Of course, you know what to do about the trunk."

"I'll set Ed on that." Wilks got out his tobacco. "I

suppose you're going to Bridgeport?"

Fellows sighed unhappily. "Somebody has to."

Fred Fellows had a session with the newspaper reporters Friday morning before he left. He told them the
victim had not been pregnant and that they hoped to
identify her soon. They did not know anything about
the man. Yes, he said, they were checking out some
clues, but he refused to say what they were. As he told
Wilks in his office after the interview, "I don't want
those guys muscling in and messing things up. Mention
that trunk and they'd be quizzing the stationmaster before Ed Lewis could get his car started."

"You didn't tell them we know who the girl is."

"They don't get that information until after her
nearest relatives. I'm not having them phone her parents until after I've talked to them. When I get back,
we'll see."

It was a sunny clear day and traffic was light on the
Merritt Parkway that morning, but the drive to Bridgeport wasn't a pleasant one for Fellows. He had delivered the news of death many times in his career as
Chief of Police, but he had never been able to develop
sufficient callousness to inure him to the pain such a
duty inevitably brought. Much as he hated ringing
strange doorbells, bearing ill news, however, it was a

task he never assigned to anyone else. Perhaps it was because it did pain him more than others, or perhaps it was a natural reluctance to assign to another a task he hated himself, but as always the trip was a torment. It was more so than usual this time, because he had not only to deliver the sad tidings to an innocent parent, but because he also had to question that parent afterwards to learn the identity of the man the girl had run off with. It was his private opinion that people in grief shouldn't be subjected to questions but, in his professional capacity, he recognized the need for speed in gaining information, even at the cost of people's feelings.

The house at 402 Westville Street was a one-family dwelling much like all the others on the block. The color was different and there was a wall holding up the embankment of lawn, but the size and shape was the same, a small two-story house with six or seven rooms.

He parked the black police station wagon in front of the walk and climbed the steps. Dressed in his leather jacket, mittens and cap, with no insignia showing, he could have been anything from a house painter to the gasman. The temperature was higher this morning, but still below freezing and Fellows dressed himself and his force for comfort rather than looks.

He rang the bell and turned his back to the door, studying the neighborhood. It was a quiet street in a quiet suburb, inhabited by quiet people who led quiet lives. But one of those inhabitants had broken out of the bonds of conformity that the identical houses spelled, had, as one of his daughters put it at dinner, "transgressed," and that one had lost her life.

The door was opened by an attractive young brunette in her late twenties, a quite pretty girl, yet stamped with a wallflower look. Her manner was quiet and efficient and capable, but she had no flair, no spark to make her stand out in the crowd. She didn't notice the police car out front or, if she did, she didn't connect it with the visitor on her porch. She looked at Fellows with a slightly challenging, quizzical expression and said politely, "Yes?"

Fellows sized her up with a trained glance that took in the cheap quality of her clothes, the lack of lipstick, the lack of a wedding ring. He said, "Is a Jean Sherman known here, miss?"

"Yes." She nodded, but was otherwise noncommittal.

"I wonder if I could speak to someone close to her. Her father, perhaps."

"My father's at work."

"Your mother?"

"She's been dead six years. What do you want?"

"Are you her sister?"

"Jean's sister?" The girl smiled. "I don't know what you're selling, mister, but you're doing it all wrong." She observed the police car now, and her eyes darted back to his face. "Something's happened. What is it?"

Fellows said, "I'm sorry. This is something I can only discuss with the Sherman family."

Her brow clouded. "Well if it's about me, I feel I have a right to know."

For once in his life, the chief was startled. "You?"

"Yes, me. I'm Jean Sherman."

"Then who—?" He stopped and started again. He introduced himself and asked to come in. He thought she paled a little at the mention of "police" and "Stockford," but at the moment he was so befuddled he wasn't sure what was happening.

She brought him into a small and comfortably furnished living room and motioned him to the couch in front of the windows. He took off his cap and waited until she sat in the facing chair before he lowered himself uneasily onto the cushions. "Now please," Jean said. "Would you tell me what this is all about?"

"Well," Fellows laughed haltingly. "Maybe you can

tell me. What do you know about a man who calls himself John Campbell?"

She paused for a moment and then said, "Nothing at all. Why?"

"You don't know anyone by that name?"

"No, I don't."

"Then tell me by what name you know the man who lives at 2 Highland Road in Stockford."

She shook her head again. "I don't know anybody in Stockford. I don't think I even know where it is."

Fellows was baffled. He found himself coming up against one blank wall after another. "Then I'll have to ask you where you were and what you were doing last weekend."

The girl licked her unrouged lips. She was nervous, but whether it was because she was lying or because she was being questioned by a policeman he couldn't be sure. "I went to New York," she said. "I spent the weekend with my sister and her husband."

"When did you go and when did you come back?"

She hesitated and stared beyond Fellows through the window. "I went down Friday night and came back Sunday night."

"And the week before—the whole week?"

"I was here. I'm always here." She leaned forward. "What's happened? What's the matter?"

"You deny ever having known a man by the name of John Campbell? Tall, medium slender, dark hair, middle thirties?"

"I do."

"Your name," the chief said, "and your address, Miss Sherman, were found written on a pad in a house rented to a John Campbell at 2 Highland Road in Stockford, which is twelve miles north of Stamford."

"I don't know how it could have got there."

Fellows leaned forward. "I don't think Mr. Campbell found it in a crystal ball, Miss Sherman. This is a serious matter. I warn you you'd better be telling the truth."

She said very evenly, "Why should I lie?"

"There are several reasons why you might. But, assuming you're telling the truth, please think carefully. Have you recently, say within the last month, met any man, never mind what his name was, who fits the description I just gave you?"

She did think, or she pretended to, but only for a couple of seconds. "I keep house for my father," she said with a trace of bitterness. "How would I get to meet any man?"

"You haven't met any men in the past month?"

"I haven't met any men in the past year."

Fellows sighed and stood up. "I'm going to have to check with your sister, Miss Sherman. You want to write out her name and address?"

"What do you have to check for? What's happened?"

"I'm sorry. I'm not at liberty to talk about it. May I have your sister's name and address please?"

"Yes, certainly." She hunted through a table drawer for paper and pencil saying, "You'll find I was there, don't worry." She scribbled rapidly, tore off the sheet, and handed it to him a bit peremptorily. She expected him to thank her and leave, but instead he studied the name and address carefully, then reached for his wallet and produced a faintly blued slip of paper with light blue writing and matched it alongside. He said, "Miss Sherman, this is just a guess, but I'd be glad to back it with a small wager that handwriting experts will be willing to get up in court and swear that these two samples were both written by the same hand."

Miss Sherman went white. "What two samples?" she whispered. "What's that other piece of writing?"

"Your name and address. The paper we found in Mr. Campbell's house."

The girl staggered slightly and clutched her throat

saying, "Oh no," as she sank back into her chair. She sat motionless staring at nothing, and the chief carefully replaced both papers and put his wallet away. Finally he said, "You want to tell me about it, Miss Sherman?"

She stirred. "No. There's nothing to tell."

Fellows made a face. He said, "Miss, either you tell me about it now, or I call the Bridgeport police and take you in. It's as simple as that. Where'd you meet Campbell?"

She started to cry a little. "On the train."

"When you went to New York?"

She nodded and fumbled for a handkerchief she didn't have. Fellows gave her his, and said, "Now don't be upset. I'm not going to bite you. Just tell me the whole thing exactly as it happened."

She cried a little more and blew her nose and clutched the handkerchief in her lap. When she spoke, she mumbled so that Fellows had to stand close to hear. "I went to a shower Friday night. One of my girl friends. I was going to New York, but this came up and I took a late train."

"What time was this train?"

"I got it here in Bridgeport at nine fifty-three. It was the William Penn. It goes to Penn Station." She dabbed at her eyes and brushed her red, wet cheeks. "I sat next to a woman who got off at Stamford and then John got on. He took her seat and we started talking. He was such a nice man, so friendly and charming. I don't know when I've met a man half as charming as he was. Not for a long long time. He was interested in me. I don't know why. I'm not the type who interests men, but he did seem to like me." She wept a little more. "I'm not a cheap flirt," she explained. "I don't go around letting strange men pick me up, but he was so nice and he invited me to go dancing with him. I couldn't. I was going to visit my sister, and I couldn't.

But he said he wanted to see me. He didn't want it to end right there." She paused and braced herself. "I didn't want it to either. I don't know any men and— I suggested that maybe he could come to my sister's, but he didn't like that. He said he wanted to see me alone, not with a lot of other people. He said we couldn't get to know each other with a lot of other people around. I didn't know what to do. I had to go to my sister's. I couldn't let her down when I was going to see her.

"And then the train came into the station and I was afraid it was all going to be over and it was going to be good-by. I was feeling pretty low because I thought —well, I don't have any boy friends and here was this wonderful, charming man, and he was going to say good-by and it would be just as though we'd never met. I thought Fate had meant us to meet and now it looked like—like the end. But he felt the same way. That's what he said. When we got off the train, he said, 'I'm not going to let it end like this,' and he said that if he couldn't take me out this evening, at least we'd have a drink before I had to go to my sister's.

"I was so glad—well, I—it meant something. He took me to some quiet cocktail lounge which was very romantic. I don't know the name of it. It was around Times Square, I think. I don't know New York very well. We talked and it was like we'd known each other all our lives and I got very bold and asked if he couldn't see me while I was visiting my sister and he said he couldn't. He had engagements and all and he asked when I was going back and when I told him Sunday night, he said he was going back Sunday too.

"And then, somehow, I don't know how it came about, he was suggesting I go back with him and go to his place. He said he'd parked his car in Stamford and he lived in Stockford and we could ride back on the train together and pick up the car and go there. Of course I knew what he was proposing and I guess I should have been horrified, but I wasn't, really. I don't mean I wanted to do anything like that, but I wasn't shocked. I said I couldn't, of course, but he was so nice I wasn't angry. The way he did it kind of made me feel flattered, because it was obvious he was a ladies' man and this was the way his mind worked and I knew he could invite dozens of girls back to his house and they'd all go, so it was really flattering that he should ask me.

"I guess I didn't say 'no' strongly enough. I wasn't mad and I just said I couldn't and then he asked why and I said I kept house for my father and he was expecting me home Sunday night and I had to get breakfast for him Monday morning before he went to work. He didn't see why my father couldn't get his own breakfast just one morning and I couldn't really either. He said I was just making excuses and that he thought I'd liked him and he must have been mistaken. I told him I did like him, but what he was proposing, well, I didn't think I ought to. He smiled and asked me if I was afraid of him. I said I wasn't, so then he told me I was afraid of life. He asked me if I'd ever had an affair before and I had to say I hadn't. It made me feel very foolish saying that because it meant I was very gauche and unattractive to men and I got red in the face and wanted to cry.

"He put his hand on mine and said that it didn't matter, that most women had had affairs by the time they'd reached my age, but that many of them had had too many affairs and it was better to have too few than to be promiscuous and have too many. I nodded and then he said that, even so, a girl ought to have one, at least. He said that time was fleeting and if I didn't grab life when I had the chance, I might miss everything and regret it as long as I lived. I didn't know what to say. Then he asked me what I was saving myself for. He already knew men didn't like me and he knew, just as I knew, that this might be the only chance

I'd ever have. He said he didn't want to persuade me to do anything against my will because it would spoil everything if I said yes and didn't mean it. He said it'd be better to say no right then and there and we'd forget the whole thing.

"The trouble was," she said, wiping her eyes again, "I didn't want it to end right then and never see him again. I didn't want to say no. He could tell I didn't, and he put his hand on mine and said I didn't have to give him an answer right then, that he'd call me at my sister's for my answer. Then he told me what it'd be like. He had this house about half an hour's drive from Stamford and if I were willing, we could take an early train back Sunday evening and go there and have supper and I could call my father and make some excuse why I wouldn't be home. We'd have dinner by candlelight and nobody would know anything because the house was out by itself away from other houses, and he'd put me on the nine o'clock train to Stamford the next morning and no one would be any the wiser. The way he said it made it sound like heaven and he was right. Nobody would ever know anything about it. There was only one thing, he said. I couldn't just agree to come. I had to want to come.

"I did want to. That was the whole trouble. I thought about it half the night at my sister's and I kept telling myself it was wrong and all, but I knew he was right. It was now or never. If I said no, I'd never see him again and if I said yes, then there might be other times and if I tried hard, he might fall in love with me. My sister got married. She's been married four years and I thought maybe I might get married."

She sighed. "He called on Saturday, right around dinnertime. I still had doubts and I was still worried. I guess it was scruples and I'd been trying so hard to fight them down. Then, when I heard his voice, so cheerful and friendly and interested, calling me 'sweet' and 'dear,' that was all I needed to decide me for keeps. I said yes, I'd go with him and we discussed it and made plans that we'd take the five forty-five train from Grand Central Sunday evening. I'd make excuses to my sister about having to get home and I wouldn't let her and her husband see me to the train and I'd meet him at the information booth in the station at five-thirty. And that's what we did."

She looked up at Fellows, red-eyed and pleading. "I know it was wrong, Mr. Fellows. I know I shouldn't have done it. I didn't know I'd get caught." She said, "Will I go to jail?"

Fellows shook his head. "Miss Sherman, if you're telling the truth, and if you co-operate with us, I doubt that anything will happen to you at all." He sat down on the couch again and got out his notebook, scribbling in it at length while Miss Sherman composed herself. Then he said, thumbing back a few pages and studying, "That address you wrote on the telephone pad. He ask you to do that?"

"Yes. I did it before we left Monday morning."

"He put you on the nine o'clock train?"

"Yes. He said he had to go to work."

"What kind of work did he do?"

She chewed her lip. "I'm not sure exactly. I think he said it was hardware. I don't know what position he held."

"Can you describe the car he drove?"

That drew a blank. Miss Sherman had no idea. "It was dark when we got in to Stamford and I guess I was nervous and excited. I didn't notice. I don't know cars anyway."

"It wasn't dark when he drove you to the train Monday morning."

"I know that, but I still don't know. I don't remember anything about the car. I don't even remember anything about the train ride."

"Was it a tan car?"

"It could have been tan or blue or purple. I can't tell you."

"What did Mr. Campbell look like?"

She looked at the chief, puzzled. "Don't you know him?"

"We know *of* him. Will you describe him, please?"

"Tall. I guess probably around six feet. I'm not good at judging height. Slender build. He wasn't fat at all." She turned pink at that remark and said quickly, "Dark hair and brown eyes, fair skin. A very good-looking man."

"How was he dressed?"

"Conservatively. When I saw him on the train he had a dark overcoat and a brown hat. Brown shoes."

Fellows referred to his notes. "Did he wear a scarf?"

"A gray wool scarf. Charcoal gray."

"Good quality clothes?"

"I don't know much about men's clothes. They looked average."

"Has he got in touch with you since Monday?"

She shook her head a little sadly. "I haven't heard from him since. He said he'd call as soon as he had the chance, but he hasn't yet."

"Can you describe his face?"

She chewed her lip again. She wanted to be helpful, but she didn't have the ability. "I thought it was a nice face, and I can close my eyes and see it just as plain, but it's hard to describe. It's a—a—" She gestured helplessly. "It's a face. Eyes, nose that looked like anybody's nose, it wasn't too big or too small, maybe his mouth was a little wider than average."

"You can't do any better than that?"

She shook her head.

"Moles? Scars? Other marks?"

"Not on his face. He had a small mole"—and here she blushed again—"on the small of his back, and another on his right shoulder blade. I don't remember anything else."

Fellows shifted his position on the couch. "Miss Sherman, are you telling me the truth when you say you have no definite plan to see him again?"

She nodded earnestly. "Yes, that's the truth."

"What did you do with your suitcases?"

"What suitcases?"

"I presume you took something to New York with you."

"Yes. Of course I did. One suitcase. I don't know what you mean, what did I do with it? I brought it home with me."

"What kind of a suitcase is it?"

"Brown—tan, I guess. It's an old one I've had for years."

"You don't own any other suitcases?"

"No. What would I need one for? I don't go anywhere, really."

"How about a green trunk?"

"You mean do I have one? I don't have any trunk."

Fellows nodded. "I see," he said and made some additional notations. "Now, Miss Sherman, I suppose while you were there you looked over the whole house?"

She hesitated. "Most of it."

"Not all of it?"

"There was one back room he kept locked. He said he used it for his office and it contained valuable papers."

"You didn't question this?"

"No. I wasn't interested in his valuable papers."

Fellows said slowly, "Miss Sherman, I hope you realize you were extremely foolish to take up with a man you knew nothing about, but I'm glad you at least had the wisdom not to be curious about his locked room."

She leaned forward, holding her hand to her breast. "What do you mean?"

"It wasn't valuable papers he kept in that room. He was keeping the dead body of another woman."

The girl came half out of the chair in horror. "No. You're fooling!"

"That's not something we fool about. And if you'd become too suspicious, Miss Sherman, I don't doubt he wouldn't have hesitated to kill you too."

Jean Sherman shrieked. She covered her face and began to scream hysterically. Fellows got up in alarm. He pulled her to her feet and shook her, but he couldn't stop her screaming. She tore at her hair until he seized her wrists and held them. The wild sounds that came from her throat reverberated through the house, jarring the walls and the crockery, paining his eardrums, making him wince. He struck her twice with his palm, striking her hard and then harder and the blows reddened her pale cheek, but otherwise had no effect. She was completely out of control. He tried to talk to her, to calm her with his voice, but nothing could be heard in the room but the peal upon peal of hysterical noise.

Finally he held her tight to control her writhing and clapped a hand over her wide mouth. It muffled her, but only until she could twist her head away and shriek again. He picked her up and carried her screaming into the nearest bedroom, laid her down, and hunted up the bathroom, cringing still at the violence of the sound. He came back with a glass of water and threw it in her face. She sputtered but only for a moment then tore at her hair and face again, emitting more piercing yells. He got a second glass and aimed it carefully. This time she choked and sat up coughing and gagging. He patted her on the back as she jerked convulsively with the effort and her face turned red.

She got her breath back and burst into tears, rolling over on the bed face down, sobbing bitterly. Fellows stood by, breathing heavily. He said, "I'm sorry, Miss Sherman. I didn't mean to upset you like that." She

kept on sobbing, but the hysteria had been broken and
Fellows turned to the bedroom window and looked out
at the house next door, wondering how much the
neighbors had heard. He expected faces at the opposite
windows and the wail of police sirens, but the house
next door looked empty and there were no faces. Perhaps no one had heard. He bit off a piece of chewing
tobacco and munched it quietly, waiting for the sobs to
stop.

It was fully fifteen minutes before Jean exhausted
herself and struggled to an elbow on the bed. Fellows
wet a washcloth in the basin and brought it in to mop
her face. She held her head steady like an obedient
child and then moaned, "I can't stand it."

He returned the washcloth and came back again. She
said, "What am I going to do?"

"I guess forget it."

"I wish I was dead."

He stood over her shaking his head. "If I were you,
Miss Sherman, I'd consider myself mighty lucky to be
alive. I wouldn't wish for anything like that."

"But he—but a murderer! How could he?"

"It takes all kinds and he's one of the rotten ones."

"I meant nothing to him. He would have killed me,
wouldn't he?"

"If he'd had to. Look, I don't think we ought to hang
around the bedroom like this. Let's go back and sit
down quietly and talk about how you're going to help
us."

"Help you?"

"That's right." He took her arm and gently urged
her off the bed. They went back to the living room and
she sat numbly again in her chair. "Why did I do it?"
she said.

"That's over and done with, Miss Sherman. Try to
forget it. The main thing is, we need your help in
catching him before he kills anybody else."

"You don't know where he is?"

"We know very little about him. He was gone when we found the body."

"Was she—who was she?"

"We don't know. We thought she was you. Will you help us?"

She nodded and said weakly, "But how?"

"Would you be willing to meet him again?"

She groaned at the thought. "I couldn't stand to see him ever again."

"The point is, he may call you. If he does, would you agree to meet him wherever he says and then call the police? You wouldn't have to go yourself. Just let the police know where he'll be, so they can go."

She brushed her cheeks. "I don't know," she said hesitantly. "I can try. But I don't think—I mean I couldn't talk to him. Even on the phone. He'd know something was wrong the minute I answered."

"Do the best you can."

She nodded. "But he wouldn't call. Not with the police looking for him."

"He might, Miss Sherman," the chief said. "Judging from what we've found out about him, he very well might."

It was early afternoon when Fellows got back to Stockford. Detective Sergeant Wilks was eating lunch at the chief's desk in the little office behind the main room, munching a sandwich and washing it down with coffee from a thermos when the chief came in.

"You get coffee on my papers," Fellows said, "and I'll skin you."

"Papers? You mean the crossword puzzle and the movie schedule and the circulars?"

"I've got your pay reports in there too." Fellows went to the chest-high windows that looked out onto the green from the ground level of the basement. The room was small with a rolltop desk and swivel chair, a wooden table, three glass-faced cabinets, and a straight chair crowded in its confines. The walls were a neutral tan and decorated with a large collection of nude calendar girls in color, the accumulation of choice selections over the years. Fellows turned from the window, glanced at the gathering of bare bosoms and flirtatious smiles overlooking the desk, and said, "Have you been eating all day, or did you get anything else done?"

"You're sounding like a man without a lunch," Wilks said, chewing. "That picture of John Campbell came in from Erie this morning. I showed it to Watly. It's not the same man."

"What about the suitcases?"

"We had a locksmith in. He opened them up for us. Nothing but odd items and women's clothes. No identification or laundry marks, and the clothes are off-the-rack things you buy in any department store. I've got the inventory list here on your desk, but it's probably lost under two feet of papers by now. Oh yes. We found a blouse with a missing button that fits the one you turned up in that back room bureau. Unger's got the suitcases out front under the desk if you want to see for yourself." Wilks swung Fellows's chair around. "Want one of my sandwiches?"

"Naw. I'm on a diet. I'm trying to give up lunch. I'll take some of your coffee, though."

"You would." Wilks drained his from the thermos cap and refilled it, handing it to the chief. "There's milk and sugar in it."

"I didn't eat breakfast, so that'll make it all right."

"Says you." Wilks watched Fellows sip it. He said, "Nope. No luck in most places. In twenty-four hours all we've found out is the identity of the victim."

"Says you," the chief retorted, hooking a leg over the edge of the table. "We don't even have that. We don't know who either of them are."

"You mean the address was a phoney?"

"Not a phoney. The girl was alive." Fellows went on to detail his interview with Jean Sherman.

Wilks whistled when he finished. "What kind of a guy is he? Are you meaning to say he killed a girl, then hopped a train for New York for the weekend and then brings another girl back to the house for the night and makes love to her in one room while the corpse is lying in the other?"

"If he killed the girl before he went to New York, that's the way it has to be."

"And how do you account for Jean Sherman being a 'J.S.'? What does he do, go through the train asking every young girl he sees what her initials are?"

"Why would he care what they are? He wouldn't be trying to set the girl up for anything."

"You mean the similarity was just a freak coincidence, huh?"

"Coincidence, but not a freak, Sid. J.S. are probably the commonest initials there are. He took the paper Jean wrote her address on with him, remember? He didn't leave it out for bait."

"If her story is true, that is."

"If it's true. Of course the alternative is something like him leaving J.S. in the house to go to New York and finding her still there when he gets back with a new lady friend. There's a fight and the victim gets it either from him or from the new girl, or from them both."

"That stinks too. You know that, don't you?"

"Sure it stinks. Doesn't life?"

Wilks said thoughtfully, "I guess no matter how you tell it, though, the initials don't matter. So it's coincidence. But what about the Sherman girl? You think she's involved more than she says?"

"I think she's telling the truth, but that's only my opinion. At any rate, I stopped off at headquarters in Bridgeport and got their help. They're standing by for a call from the girl at any time and they're also putting a watch on her house just in case Campbell decides to come see her."

Wilks snorted. "Come and see her? That's a laugh."

"He's got her address."

"And he's got his name in the papers too. You don't think he's going to walk into that trap?"

"It's not in the papers much. It made headlines around here, and it got an item on the front page in Bridgeport and New Haven, but this isn't the kind of story they follow up on—not unless the body turns out to be somebody important. Jean Sherman never even saw it in the paper."

"I still say he'd never try it. He's not going to take that chance."

Fellows said, "But we aren't going to pass up that chance either. We need Bridgeport's help in finding out about the girl. It's part of the whole thing, checking her out and seeing if her alibi stands up."

"You mean if she went to New York as she says?"

The chief nodded. "And what she was doing the rest of this month. Let's face it, this bluebeard technique is a little too fiendish to sound real. She might know Campbell better than she lets on—and that's another reason for keeping her under surveillance." He finished the coffee and returned the thermos cap. "MacFarlane call today?"

"Nope. Not yet."

Fellows reached to the desk for the phone. "Let's hope he's got something by now."

When MacFarlane was finally on the line, he sounded apologetic. "I don't mean to keep you waiting, but it wasn't an easy job, Fred. I'm still writing the report."

"Don't make me wait for the mails, Jim. Give it to me now."

"Yes, well, I'm sorry to say I just don't know the cause of death. Whatever it was it must have been inflicted on parts of the body that are missing. She could have died from a blow on the head or strangulation."

"It wasn't natural causes, then?"

"Not in the body itself. She could have had a brain hemorrhage or something like that, but it was probably accident or murder. It might even have been suicide by hanging. I can't tell you."

"Is there anything you can tell me?"

"I can estimate her age for you. About thirty. And she's never had a child and she wasn't pregnant."

"You told me that last night."

"Yes. As I said, a crude attempt was made to remove the organs affected, but it wasn't entirely successful. As for the time of death, that's been very hard to determine, but I have reduced the limits."

"What are they down to now?"

"Some time between Friday afternoon and Saturday evening. It was some time in that thirty-hour period."

Fellows said his thanks and hung up. "That woman," he told Wilks, "was dead in his house before he went to New York if Jean's telling the truth. She was lying in that back bedroom when he brought her home with him."

"I didn't know anybody got that hard up."

"It makes me change my mind about him."

"In what way?"

"We thought maybe this amateur butcher gave up destroying the body because he couldn't stomach the task. It must be for another reason. Anyone who could kill a woman and weekend in New York and come back with another woman, anybody who'd have nerve to bring a woman into the house he's hiding a body in, he's not going to get queasy cutting the body up."

"That doesn't help tell us who he is."

"No, but we're starting to get a picture of the guy. We're learning what he's like."

"That's more of your mumbo jumbo. All this theorizing doesn't get us anywhere. Facts are what you need, Fred, facts and data and that reminds me. I did a few other things this morning I should tell you about. We collected all the dust in the house and shipped it to Hartford. And I fingerprinted the silver for you. You were right on that, Fred. I did get some prints from it. They're on their way to Hartford too. Cassidy's taking them up."

"What about the grocery boy Mrs. Banks saw talking to Campbell? And what about the trunk?"

"Ed is tracking down the trunk business. I've got two others canvassing the grocers."

"And the knife and saw?"

"What about them?"

"I thought you were the 'fact' man, Sid. They were bought weren't they? Somebody sold them to Campbell. It would help if we knew where."

"O.K., O.K., I get it. You want your seat back." Wilks crumpled his sandwich wrappings together and stuffed them into the paper bag his lunch had come in. He thrust them into the wastebasket under the desk.

Fellows said, "And, Sid. On the theory side of the ledger, the more you can find out what the man is like, the better chance you have of finding him."

"You aren't telling me anything. The trouble is we don't know what he's like. Only that he's got dark hair, is fairly tall, moderately slender, dresses well, has a fair amount of money, and plays around with women. That fits a lot of people, Fred."

"We know more than that. For instance, we can figure he's married and I would guess he lives in a neighboring town."

Wilks showed interest. "How did you dream that bit up and why?"

"We guess he's married because of the assumed name, of course. But he wouldn't be living in Stockford, that's pretty sure. Stockford's too small a town for a man to change his name and set up a love nest without getting caught at it. On the other hand, he wouldn't want to travel too far, would he? Besides that, Mrs. Banks had him pegged as coming to the house every night about half past five and then he'd leave and come back later, about eight, and leave again between ten and eleven. Know what that sounds like? He finishes work, picks up some groceries, drives out to the love nest, goes home to wherever he lives for dinner, then comes back to the love nest in the evening."

"Nice of his wife to be so permissive."

"He's got to have an excuse to go out, of course."

"Go out every night, you mean. That's stretching an excuse pretty thin."

Fellows took a chew of tobacco. "I've been thinking about that, Sid. He might pretend he has to work."

"Some job. Long hours and no income."

"The guy would have to work for himself. That's the way I see it. He's got a store or something and pretends he has to go back after supper to catch up on the books."

"Every night?"

"He only rented the house for a month. He can pretend it's a busy period. He fell behind at Christmas and is trying to catch up. He'll be tied up evenings for a month."

Wilks tilted his chair back and stared absently at the glamour girls on the wall. "And I suppose hopping a train to New York for the weekend is also business. That's not a wife you've got him married to, it's a door mat."

Fellows said ruefully, "I guess I forgot that."

"The trouble with you is you operate too high up in the stratosphere. You ought to reason from the facts and stop reasoning from the reasoning. You'll end up in outer space."

"I've got to figure this guy out, Sid, and we don't have many facts to work from."

"But you'll probably figure him out wrong. This isn't a Sherlock Holmes story. Old Sherlock could see scratches on the inner side of Watson's shoes and reason they were made by a knife scraping mud off and reason from that that a wife would be more careful and decide he had a careless maid and he'd got his feet wet and caught cold. In real life, you'd probably find he slipped off a curb and scratched his shoe and he doesn't have a maid, isn't married, and never caught cold in his life."

Fellows chewed quietly for a bit. Then he said. "Let's

see, Sid. You owe me two dollars and a quarter from cribbage. I'll bet you double or nothing John Campbell or whatever his name is, doesn't live in Stockford, but lives in a town not too far away."

Wilks grinned. "You throw in that he's also married and owns a store and I'll take it."

"No, thanks. On that I won't bet."

"On the other I'm not betting either." Wilks got up. "You're going to have to lose your dough at cribbage, Fred."

Friday afternoon the Erie police, at Fellows's request, initiated the task of checking out all friends of Vice President John Campbell of the Gary Hardware Company and all men who worked or had worked there. While it was possible that the man they wanted had picked the name Campbell by accident, Fellows thought it more likely the choice had been deliberate. If so, it was made by someone who knew a John Campbell held a position in that company. It was the Erie police's job to track down those who might.

The New York police also had a job. Theirs was the relatively more simple task of discovering if a "John Campbell" had registered in any hotels on the evening of Friday, February twentieth.

At four o'clock that afternoon, Town Prosecutor Leonard Merrill had a session with Fellows in his office. Judge Cobbitt Reed had called an inquest for ten o'clock the following morning and the prosecutor wanted all the facts in the case. "Get him to postpone it," Fellows said. "We don't know anything yet. We won't have enough evidence tomorrow morning for a flea to stumble over. What kind of an inquest will that be? We don't even know how the girl died."

"I can't postpone it," Merrill said. "The judge is going on vacation. In fact, he's having to hold up his departure for the inquest. He's not happy about things at all."

"I guess none of us are." The chief then explained all they had done and tried to do so far. "One thing," he said. "I don't want this Jean Sherman girl brought into it. I'm telling you, but don't you tell anybody else."

"What do you mean? I've got to tell the judge. I've got to bring it up. I can't hold out at the inquest."

"Then you make sure it's a private inquest. I don't want anybody to know about her."

Merrill shook his head. "Since when are you starting to worry about girls' reputations, Fred? What are you trying to protect her for?"

"I'm using her for bait."

"He's not going to bite. You know that."

"There's a chance, Len. There's always a chance. A guy who'll dare bring her to the murder house will dare see her while he's on the run. A guy like him can't leave women alone. He may not be able to leave this woman alone—unless we tip him off we know about her."

Merrill admitted the chief had a point. "All right, we'll play it your way. She's getting a break she doesn't deserve, but we won't give out her name. I'll talk to the judge."

Fellows smiled. "If you're getting moral on me, she got her punishment when she found out what he was. She doesn't need any more."

"All right. I said we wouldn't use her. But I'm going to need more—a lot more. You don't have anything here."

"I told you that, Len."

Merrill made a face. "Reed's going to think I'm a fool when I go through this tomorrow. Well, I'll take these reports along and anything else that comes in, you get to my house tonight. I've got to work this into something."

When the town prosecutor went out, Fellows was ac-

costed by Hilders, the *Courier* reporter and the only one
in headquarters that afternoon. He said, "What's the
bellow, Fellows?"

"No reports in since the last statement, Mr. Hilders."

Hilders leaned on the duty desk, cramping Sergeant
Gorman. "Just call me John, Chief. And cough up.
Don't give me that nothing-to-report gag. My paper
wants news."

"I thought you were out making your own news, Mr.
Hilders?"

"I was looking around. I didn't find anything."

"We haven't found anything either."

Hilders got conspiratorial. "Now look, Chief, this
case has got juice in it. A girl's living with a man. He
murdered her. Come on, there's meat there. That's a
story, a big story. Sure, you know things you haven't
told the press. You're following leads, but you know
something about those two people. You know dirt
about them. That's what my paper wants, the dirt."

"The dirt, as you call it, you're going to have to look
up yourself. That's not our department. We're looking
for information about her death. That's all we're looking for and that's all we're going to make statements
about around here." The chief went to his office and
turned at the door. "Right now, we don't have any reports." He closed the door and didn't come out again.

At five after five that afternoon the first results came
in. Patrolman David Lerner, checking hardware stores
in plainclothes, armed with a burnt knife and saw,
called in to announce that the knife, and presumably
the saw too, had been purchased at Cutler's Hardware
Store on Bishop Street.

"The saw could have been bought anywhere," he
told the chief in his office. "It's stocked by most of the
stores, but the knife, that's a brand only Cutler's car-
ries. That's what I was told the fourth place I went,
and Cutler's confirms it. That's their knife, all right,

but they don't remember when they sold it or who bought it."

"They write out sales slips?"

"I don't know, Chief. I didn't ask them about that. I only asked if they could tell me when it was sold—if they had any record. They said they didn't."

Fellows picked up his phone and called them. They didn't make out sales slips, they told him. Everything was cash over the counter.

"How much would a knife and saw like that come to?" the chief asked.

"The knife is two and a quarter and that particular saw sells for two seventy-five. Five dollars even. That's not counting the sales tax."

"How about checking through your files for purchases of exactly five dollars for us? We might be able to pinpoint it that way."

"We don't have any files, Chief."

Fellows made a face. "Come on, now. Your cash register totals up your purchases, doesn't it? It turns out slips, doesn't it?"

The manager laughed. "We don't have a cash register. We have a cash drawer. We start in the morning with twenty dollars in change in the drawer and at the end of the day we add up what we've got and subtract twenty to get our daily intake. I can tell you the total amount of money we took in on any given day, but I couldn't tell you any individual purchases."

Fellows hung up. He said sadly, "You wait all day for a break and when you get it, it doesn't do you a damned bit of good."

The next report, however, promised more. Patrolman Harris called in from Peck's grocery store on Williams Street. "Chief, this place delivered an order to Campbell on Friday the thirteenth. The boy isn't in right now. He's out delivering, but he'll be back in a little while." To Fellows it was a chance to escape from his office. He said, "You hold him there. I'm coming out," and hung up the phone.

Peck's was a small, dingy store occupying the first floor of a frame house that, in other respects, resembled the rest of the frame houses that lined both sides of the street. It was a private operation unconnected with the chains and catered to the neighborhood because of its convenience and because it made deliveries. Mr. Peck, a short, fat, bald-headed man with glasses and an apron soiled with the day's doings, was waiting on a woman customer who kept eyeing patrolman Harris when Fellows opened the glass-paned front door and came in.

"My boy ain't back yet," Mr. Peck said, putting the woman's groceries into a brown paper bag. "You gotta wait."

Fellows waited. He opened a bag of potato chips and fed Harris and himself from it until the woman left. Then he laid a half a dollar on the counter and waited for his change. "You say the name was Campbell? The Campbell who lived at 2 Highland Road?"

"That's the one. Yup."

"How many deliveries did you make to them?"

"Just that one."

"Mr. Campbell ever shop here?"

"Not that I know of."

"You know all your customers?"

"Most of 'em."

"This one would be about six feet tall, middle thirties, wearing a tan or a dark coat, slender build. He'd do his shopping after five o'clock."

"Can't remember anybody like that."

A blue and battered panel truck turned from the street and rattled into the drive alongside the house to the back. There was a banging of the truck's loose rear doors and a youth came in the back way wearing an apron, blue jeans, and a quilted cloth jacket. He was lugging a wooden crate of empty bottles and a couple of cardboard cartons in red, raw hands.

There was a room out back behind the store proper. Its floor was rough and unswept and cartons, opened and sealed, were stacked against the walls. The chief and Harris were waiting for him there and Fellows said, "We're police officers. What's your name, son?"

"Who, me? Andy, sir. Andy Palekowski." He was short and thin with a shock of tousled dark hair and a small wizened face. He dumped the crates and rubbed his red hands.

"Mr. Peck tells me you delivered groceries to a party named Campbell two weeks ago today. You remember anything about it?"

His eyes widened. "Geez. That's the dame that got killed, ain't it? I was telling Mr. Peck I almost got to see her."

"You remember the delivery?"

He nodded eagerly. "Sure I remember it. I gave the stuff to the guy who killed her. He paid me. He touched my hands. He touched them with the hands he killed her with."

Fellows smiled wanly. "I hope you washed them, son."

"Yeah. Huh? Are you kidding me?"

The chief put a foot on one of the nearby cartons. "No, I'm not kidding you. What we want you to do is tell us everything you can remember. You can remember that far back all right?"

"Sure, why not? It's the only delivery I ever made there. I had to go way out to do it. So when I turned the corner, this guy Campbell, he'd just pulled his car in the drive. I'd have gone around to the back like I usually do, but he was blocking the drive and I pulled up in front. So I'm getting my stuff out and he's getting out of the car and he sees I'm going to make a delivery, so he comes over and says something like, 'This for

Campbell?' or something like that and I tell him, 'Yeah,' so he says he'll take them and how much is it? Well, I tell him it's—I forget what—but whatever it is, he takes out his wallet and pays me and he gives me the exact change and a tip and the last I see of him, he's carrying the box into the house."

"What'd the man look like? Remember?"

"Sure. I remember pretty good. Kind of a happy-go-lucky type. Kinda tall and dark and smiling. I don't know the color of his eyes, but he was well built. He was in shirt sleeves, dark brown pants. Not bad-looking. And I guess he was in his thirties somewhere. He looked like he'd been around."

Fellows said, "I guess he had. What about the car? Remember that?"

The boy fished in his jacket pocket for a cigarette to augment his sense of importance. "You can bet I do," he said. "When it comes to cars, that's something I know real well. This one was a 1957 Ford two-door sedan." He lighted the cigarette with a Zippo, snapped it shut, and closed his eyes. "Blue plates," he added, remembering. "Connecticut all right. Tan car, and dented left rear fender." He looked again at Fellows. "How's that?"

"That's good, Andy. That's very good. You'd know this guy if you saw him again?"

"Yeah. I'd know him. And I'd know his car. You bring him around and I'll identify him for you."

"We'll bring him around, son. You'll get your chance."

Plainclothesman Ed Lewis was waiting in the main room of headquarters, talking to Wilks and Sergeant Gorman, when Fellows and Harris got back. The chief pulled off his cap and unzipped his jacket and said, "Jesus, Ed, I thought you died or something."

"I've been collecting information, Chief."

"You ought to have the encyclopedia by now. Gorman," Fellows told the sergeant, "get out and get some coffee, will you? I'm hungry and cold."

"You want a sandwich to go with it?"

Wilks said, "Just get him coffee. He's on a diet."

"Coffee and cigarettes," Fellows said. "It's great for the weight."

Gorman went out, and Fellows stripped off his jacket and sat down. "How is it, Ed? Good?"

"I think it is." Lewis took out a notebook and flipped the pages. "First I went to the railroad station. They remembered the trunk and the girl. You know that town five miles south of Ashmun?"

"Townsend?"

"Yeah. Well, that's where the trunk was shipped from. It was checked through on the girl's ticket and came in on February second. That's Monday. It was delivered to the house that afternoon. I hunted up the guy who made the delivery and that took a little time. He remembered it, but he didn't have much to tell. He took it to the girl's house and put it in the cellar for her, right where we found it."

"He tell you what the girl was like?"

"Yep. About five-six and a half, a hundred and thirty pounds or so. He couldn't guess her weight too well, just said she was built right for her height, not fat, not thin. The description fit the body, or what we know of the body. She had dark hair, looked about thirty, like MacFarlane says she was, rather pretty, but kind of hard. Not tough looking, but like a girl who knew her way around."

"Like it wasn't the first time she'd been with a man?" suggested the chief.

"Like it wasn't even the second."

"What else?"

"Well, as I say, the trunk arrived on the second, but the girl, she arrived on Sunday the first. I talked to the cab drivers. A driver named Dan Pettigrew remembered taking her out to the house that day. He wasn't sure of the day until he checked his records, but that's when it was, and he remembers the whole thing. She came in on the twelve-thirty train, which made a stop at Townsend at twelve-fifteen. Pettigrew remembers her because she was the only person who got off and she had two suitcases which she took with her across the street to the Bar-Ritz lunch counter, where she had a sandwich. She was wearing, he said, a fur coat and a tailored suit which was dark blue or black."

Fellows said, "Which we found in her trunk, right, Sid?"

"There was a fur and a dark suit."

Lewis nodded. "I checked the lunch counter and they don't remember her, but that doesn't mean anything. She came out again with the suitcases and took

Pettigrew's cab. He drove her out and talked to her some. She was polite, but she didn't talk more than she had to. She admitted she was new in town and she and her husband were going to live at the place for three months while he was assigned to this territory. He tried to pump her—"

"Three months?" Fellows interrupted.

"That's what she told him."

"But the house was only rented for one month." Fellows rubbed his chin. "I guess this man Campbell was snowing that girl right down the line."

"Sounds like it, Chief," Lewis answered. "For one thing, she told the cab driver he was in the hardware business, representing this territory. That's what he told the real estate guy."

"Hardware," Fellows mused. "That occupation keeps coming up."

"I think that's where we're going to find our man, Chief. He's going to be in hardware someplace."

"I wonder if he owns a hardware store," Fellows said thoughtfully.

"Cutler's?" put in Wilks.

The chief smiled. "You can check it out, Sid. Go on, Ed."

"That's all Pettigrew got out of her, Chief. Hardware and three months. He took her bags to the front door for her and she paid him off and let herself in and that was that."

"She had a key, then?"

"Yeah. Campbell must've given it to her."

"I don't get it," Fellows grumbled. "If he's in contact with the girl right along, why does he rent a house for her? What's wrong with the place she's already living at?"

"She's got a family or something," Wilks suggested.

"So what's a family? They go to bed, don't they? Besides, how's she going to explain going off like that to a family? He sets her up in a house, not to live with her, but to visit her evenings, which he could do wherever she already was living. There's only one reason I can see for that. He must have planned to kill her all along. She probably told him she was pregnant and he wanted to get rid of her."

Lewis said, "I thought MacFarlane said she wasn't pregnant."

Fellows shrugged. "That doesn't stop her from telling him she is, does it?"

"No. I guess you're making sense, Chief."

"Am I? Why does the girl take the house? Why does she give up what she's got and go into this weird setup?"

Wilks laughed. "Come on, Fred. Haven't you ever heard of a girl getting set up in an apartment a boy friend pays the rent on?"

"Yep. That I have. But not for three months, or one month, or whatever. That's like the art collector who paid a thousand bucks to an Eskimo sculptor for a hunk of carving he fancied, only when it arrived at his house, it was nothing but a pail of water because the Eskimo worked in ice. I mean, what's this girl buying?"

Nobody had an answer and Fellows shrugged his shoulders. "All right. I guess we'll have to let whoever knew the girl answer that one. You get anything more, Ed?"

Lewis nodded. "Oh yes. A lot more. I didn't know why a girl who lived in Bridgeport would be shipping her trunk from Townsend—"

"That wasn't the girl," Fellows said.

"So Sid told me, but back then I was wondering, and I checked on it anyway. Well, they remembered her on account of not many trunks get shipped out of Townsend. The stationmaster looked over the files and found the girl brought it in Saturday about noon. That's the last day of January. She filled in the label in front of him and he stuck it on the trunk and put it aside for shipment. That was all he could tell me, but I asked the porter at the station and he said it was brought there by this girl and a man in a pick-up truck. And get this. The man was dark-haired, fairly tall, medium build, and he was wearing work clothes. He and the girl both came in the truck and they seemed friendly. The guy got the porter to help him unload it and take it inside where the girl filled out the label and then the two of them got back in the pick-up and drove away."

"Anything else in the back of that pick-up, Ed?"

"No, but I asked him about that truck and he said it was dusty like it had been used to carry cement."

"Construction worker, huh?"

"Sounds like it. His work pants were dusty too."

"Any name on the side of the truck?"

"The porter thought so, but he couldn't remember what it was."

Gorman returned with coffee and the men chipped in. They took their paper containers and tested for flavor, and Fellows said, "Got anything else?"

Lewis said, "How the hell much more do you want?"

"Well, I wouldn't mind having the name of the man and the name of the girl. That would help."

"The woman's name was Campbell, according to the stationmaster."

"Great." Fellows swigged some of his coffee. "Well, we'd better see what we've got before that reporter Hilders comes back from supper. One thing. I don't want any of you people giving out interviews. Any reporter ask you something, even if it's about the weather, you refer him to me. I don't want the papers knowing anything I don't want them to know."

Wilks said, "What things don't you want them to know?"

"I don't want them knowing about that tan Ford

and what we're going to do about it. I don't want any-body knowing anything about the Sherman girl." He fondled his cup and sat up straighter. "We've got leads to both the man and the girl. If we can find out who just one of them was, then we should have no trouble finding the identity of the other. We're going to explore both ends and see if we can't come out in the middle. Tomorrow we're going to hit the Motor Vehicle Department for a list of all tan 1957 Fords in the state. Meanwhile, every available man is going to be put on tracking that car. It had a dented rear fender, so I want every garage south as far as Stamford, north as far as Danbury, west to the state line, and east to Bridgeport canvassed to see if any repair work was done on such a fender. In addition, we're going to hit all service stations, starting in Stockford and fanning out, for customers owning tan Fords. One way or another we're going to find that car. Now I don't want any leaks. I don't want the murderer reading about what we're doing. I don't want him painting that car or running it into the Sound.

"As for the girl, the evidence is that she lives in Townsend and I'd guess the man probably lives there too. In either case, we shouldn't have too much trouble. It's a small town. I'll want three men checking Townsend service stations tomorrow morning. Meanwhile, Wilks and I'll try to find the girl. If we're good and lucky, and we should be, we ought to have the man in jail by tomorrow night."

The chief finished his coffee and stood up. "All right. You men can go home now. I'm going to write up a statement for the press. If the morning papers announce that our J.S. came from Townsend, we may have help finding out who J.S. really is." He snapped his fingers. "Hey, Gorman. Get on the phone to the Townsend police. Ask Chief Ramsey if anybody's been reported missing from there."

When the chief drove home at seven o'clock, he wore a smile of carefully controlled, but not completely contained optimism. True, Ramsey had reported no known missing persons but that didn't surprise Fellows. The girl with the initials J.S. had expected a three months' stay in the murder house and she would have made the necessary excuses to her friends and relatives. That was nothing compared to the credit side of the ledger. The papers had been given the news and it would appear in the morning editions. The victim had been pinpointed as coming from a town of 2500 people and that made tracing her easy. Fellows was willing to bet the man was from there too and if he was, it wouldn't take long to uncover him. Things, the chief decided, were progressing nicely.

By the time the inquest started Saturday morning, activities were already well under way at Police Headquarters. Dzanowski, Harris, and Raphael had gone to Townsend to canvass filling stations and work south. Chernoff, Wade, and Kettleman were covering Stockford, Ashmun, and between points as far as Townsend. Four more men were working the towns to the north, east, and west. The local police of all towns in the area between Stamford, Danbury, and Bridgeport had been alerted to watch for a tan, 1957 Ford with a dented rear fender.

The inquest itself took place in the conference room of Judge Reed on the first floor of the town hall. Present at the hearing were Town Prosecutor Merrill, Dr. MacFarlane, Wilks, and Fellows and the session lasted only half an hour. MacFarlane's testimony was in substance the same as his report to Fellows. The dead girl was about thirty, brunette, estimated height five feet six, estimated weight 135 pounds. She had died sometime between Friday afternoon, February twentieth, and Saturday evening, February twenty-first. The woman was not pregnant, had never borne a child, and the cause of death was impossible to determine due to the fact parts of the body were missing. He produced a series of glossy prints of the dismembered remains and showed them around to substantiate this point. Judge Reed glanced at them quickly and looked away, Merrill looked at them briefly, and Fellows didn't bother looking at them at all.

When it was the chief's turn, he told what had been accomplished in the case so far. The man in question was not the John Campbell of the Gary Hardware Company. The victim was not Jean Sherman in Bridgeport. Campbell could be identified by three different people, he drove a tan Ford with Connecticut plates, and his description was known. "Watly and the boy, Andy," Fellows said, "are going to Hartford this afternoon to look through their photo gallery. If the man's ever been arrested in this state, we should be able to get a line on him."

Judge Reed, unhappy at having to delay his vacation in the first place, was even more disgruntled over what he'd had to delay it for. When Merrill had finished his questioning, Reed said, "What kind of an inquest is this? What kind of a decision am I supposed to hand down on the information you've given me? You've had the body for two days and you don't even know how she died. You don't even know who she is or who took the knife to her."

Fellows said, "That's right, Judge."

Reed fixed him with a stony eye. "I would say it behooves you, Chief, to get yourself some help. The Stockford police department is obviously ill-equipped to handle major crimes. Why haven't you called in the State Police?"

"We have. We've been using their facilities right along, their lab and technicians. And they're helping us hunt for Campbell's car."

"I would strongly recommend, Chief, that you turn the whole investigation over to them."

Fellows said, "Is that your verdict, Judge?"

"Don't be flip."

"And don't you be telling me my business, Judge."

"I'm not trying to." Reed looked at his watch impatiently and said, "I can't give you a verdict. All I can say right now is that a woman died from unknown causes and was mutilated after death by an unknown man. What this court wants is the cause of death and the identity of the man." He said, as an afterthought, "And the identity of the woman." He scraped his chair back and stood up.

"Have a good time in Florida," Fellows said.

The judge left the room to go back to his chambers and the others went out into the hall where Carleton Lawrence, editor of the Stockford *Weekly Bulletin*, the reporter named Hilders, and two other newspapermen were waiting. Merrill gave them the inquest verdict and MacFarlane said to the chief, "How long do I have to keep the body? When do we bury her?"

"How long can you hold off?"

"As long as I have to, I suppose."

"Call me on Monday, Jim. I want to find out who she is if I can."

The chief went downstairs to headquarters and Hilders followed him. "Hey, Chief, how about letting me take a look around the murder house?"

Fellows said, "Help yourself."

"It's locked. Restlin has the keys."

"Then ask him. We're through with it. It's not our house."

"I have asked him. He won't open it up."

The chief pulled open the hall door to the main room for Wilks and himself and held it so Hilders could follow. He said to Sergeant Unger, "Any reports?"

"One from Erie." He handed it to the chief who read, PRELIMINARY INVESTIGATION REVEALS SIX MEN WHO

ONCE WORKED FOR GARY HARDWARE NOW LIVING IN CONNECTICUT-NEW YORK AREA STOP HARVEY BENTON 228 WESTSIDE STREET, HARTFORD, JAMES COLES 164 EDGE-HILL ROAD, STRATFORD, MARTIN FINE 55 WEYMOUTH LANE, NEW ROCHELLE, RICHARD LESTER, LAST KNOWN IN STAMFORD, KIRBY NORRIS 681 BEVERLY DRIVE, NEW HAVEN, SAMUEL TRAUBE 40 ESSEX STREET, NEW LONDON.

Fellows showed it to Wilks and said, "Nobody in Townsend. I guess that was expecting too much."

Hilders wanted to see it, but Fellows kept it away. "You don't want names, Mr. Hilders. It's just people who know a John Campbell works for Gary Hardware. Their names are our business."

"Everything's your business. I can't write a story on the handouts you give."

"I thought you were going to nose around on your own, Mr. Hilders."

"You've got me blocked. You won't let me into the murder house, for instance."

"There's nothing there in the first place and it's not our affair in the second."

"That's what you say. All right, then, since you're so co-operative, who's the girl in the case?"

"We don't know."

"I don't mean the victim, I mean the other girl."

Fellows turned around a little too quickly for casual innocence. "What other girl?"

"I've heard rumors," Hilders said. "There's another girl in that house, isn't there? He had two women."

"Where'd you get that story?"

Hilders leered slightly. "You know I'm not going to reveal my sources, Chief."

"If you've been pumping my men—"

"I'd be doing my job," Hilders pulled out his pad. "Let's have the rest of it, Chief. What's her name?"

Fellows's face got flinty. He said, "There's no story of any girl, and you'd better not try to print any."

Hilders grinned and repocketed the pad. "In that case, then, maybe you wouldn't mind calling old man Restlin and getting him—"

"A little blackmail, Mr. Hilders?"

The reporter flushed. "No. Nothing like that, Chief. One good turn."

Fellows pointed a finger and said, stressing his words, "I'm going to tell you something, boy. You play along with me and I'll give you everything I can, newswise. But you just once print something against my wishes and the only news you'll get on this case is what you steal from other papers."

Hilders made a face, but he didn't say anything. Fellows waited for a couple of seconds to give him a chance, then turned to Unger. "You get the word around. No cop is to speak to any reporter. No one!" Then he said more evenly, "As for that stuff from Erie, get the headquarters in each town to check those names out. Wilks and I are going to Townsend to run down a clue."

The temperature was above freezing for the first time in a week when the chief and Wilks got to Townsend. The thermometer on the Fizz-Rite soft-drink signboard in the outskirts read thirty-three degrees against its background of bare trees and gray sky. It might be the end of the last freeze before spring and Wilks said so hopefully as they pulled into town.

Police Headquarters was a small, converted frame house on the main road. There was a flag waving briskly from a pole in the front lawn and a sign on a post on the veranda. Fellows and Wilks parked at the curb out front and went along the tarred walk, up the steps, and over the wide wooden porch. The front door opened into a narrow hall to a drinking fountain and rooms in the rear. In the wall at the left was a half door with a flat top on it forming a desk while shutting off the police records room beyond. Another room on the right was the chief's office and Chief Delbert Ramsey was eating a hot lunch sent from a chili parlor across the street. He was a small, sour man with the reputation of a tyrant and if he didn't smile when the two officers came in, the fact that he didn't scowl

meant he was glad to see them. "Well, come in," he
said, and glanced at the old pendulum clock with Ro-
man numerals on the opposite wall. "It's ten after
twelve. You had lunch?"

Fellows said, "I hadn't even thought of it," while
shaking the limp thin hand the chief held out as a matter of formality.

"You oughtta eat," Ramsey said. "This crap is lousy,
but it's hot. Raises hell with my ulcer. You got an ulcer, Fellows?"

"Not yet. I'd like to have you meet Detective Sergeant Wilks."

Ramsey gave Wilks a curt nod. "That's 'cause you
got an eighteen-man force. You try to work with six
sometime. Take last night. Accident on the highway.
Two people killed. I got five men and myself. Two of
them and me were up till after two in the morning.
You can send somebody else, but I got to show up in
person and look at all that blood. Why don't I send out
for some chili for you and I'll tell you about it. Two
teen-agers went off the road and wrapped themselves
around a tree. It was a mess."

Fellows said, "We could do with a sandwich, I
guess."

Ramsey snapped at the open door, "Hey, you, Hayes.
C'mere."

The man on the desk came in, was given orders, and
headed out across the street. Ramsey said, "See? He
goes across the street and there's nobody at the desk.
What can you do with five men?"

The two Stockford policemen took chairs and
watched Ramsey gulp more of his chili. Fellows said,
"We're still trying to identify the body we found. Her
trunk was sent from here."

"I told you we ain't got anybody missing, Fellows."

"I didn't think you would. She'd make plans to be
away."

"So what are you going to do?"

"Check all the 'S's. Does Townsend have a town directory?"

Ramsey snorted. "This town ain't got enough dough to pay its police chief a decent salary. I sweat, with a bunch of crumbs for cops, and get peanuts. We work extra hours like last night. There ain't no dough for a directory."

Fellows sighed. "Then it's the telephone book, I guess."

"What're you gonna do? Call up all the people whose names start with 'S'?"

"That's the general idea, I guess."

"I hope you ain't gonna want any of my men to help you. I only got five, you know."

"We'll handle it ourselves. Maybe we could make the calls from here."

Ramsey made a face. "I suppose so. I guess you can use our phones. I got two in the other room. I hope it won't take you long. I don't like my wires being tied up."

"There shouldn't be too many 'S's in a town of twenty-five hundred people."

"More 'S's than anything else, I guess. Now if it was 'Z,' we only got three."

"Be nice if it was." Fellows got up again. "Maybe we could start now."

Ramsey let Wilks and the chief find their own way to the phones. He had finished his meal and was dumping a pill from a bottle into his hand.

Fellows and Wilks started with the three female J.S.'s listed in the phone book, Joan Steckle, Jessica Smith, Jennifer Sandhurst. That brought no results, so they next tried the two names that were preceded only by the initial 'J'. After that they started alphabetically, Wilks at the top and Fellows at the bottom, calling families, asking the number of persons in each, asking if any female member had left town on or around the first of February.

It was a long and thankless task and the sandwiches Hayes brought them were long gone before they were through. It was a fruitless task too. There was no call that even showed promise. No one they talked to knew anything about a girl leaving town at the beginning of the month, and in the whole list, they failed to get an answer only three times.

They finished at ten after three, thanked Ramsey and went across the street to the chili parlor for some coffee. It was strong coffee with a bitter taste, as if it had been made with yesterday's grounds, but it suited their mood. "I feel like we're chasing a shadow," Wilks grumbled. "It's got me wondering maybe she borrowed the luggage and her initials haven't got a 'J' or an 'S' in them. Or maybe she comes from some other place. The guy in the truck can only carry her trunk to here and she has to ship it the rest of the way."

Fellows blew gently on his coffee. "I don't think it's that bad, Sid. We got three no-answers. It might be one of them."

"I've got a very strong feeling it's not. It's a better feeling you might say."

"They've got to be her suitcases and trunk, Sid. Who're you going to borrow a suitcase from for three months?—pretty new suitcases too?" He sipped his coffee and mused. "And that truck driver. He couldn't be the man, could he?"

"He fits the description."

Fellows shook his head. "But if he's got a truck, and she's got the trunk, why ship it? Stockford's not more than a twenty-minute ride. Why didn't he take it to the house?"

"Easy. He doesn't want to be seen with her."

"That may be, but how would he explain that to the girl?"

"You mean you think the truck driver isn't the guy?"

Fellows shrugged. "I don't know who he is. But let's get back to the girl. We've got to presume her initials are J.S., there's no other way around it. And I'd have to believe she comes from here. I can't see sending the trunk from here otherwise, your explanation to the contrary notwithstanding."

"Then why don't we find somebody who knows her?"

Fellows sipped some more coffee and got out his chewing tobacco. "That's what we have to figure. All right, a single girl. She gets around so she must have access to a phone. The phone, unless it belongs to one of the no-answers, isn't in the family name. So she doesn't live with her family. That makes it a boarding house or she shares an apartment with another girl and it's in the other girl's name. That make sense to you, Sid?"

"Yeah. So do we call every number in the book?"

"I don't think we'd have to do that. Now why would a single girl live in a town like this without her family?"

"She works in it."

"Exactly. And the biggest company in town is the Graystone Greeting Card Company. What do you want to bet she doesn't, or didn't work there?"

Wilks smiled for the first time. "Let's see if we can find out."

They left the chili parlor with an optimistic step, but they weren't to gain the information that day. The Graystone Greeting Card Company was shut down for the weekend and attempts to locate someone with access to the files was a failure.

When they abandoned that hunt, they tried the three phone numbers that hadn't answered before and, getting no answer again, went out to each house and ques-

tioned the neighbors. Again they came up against a
blank wall. No departed girl was connected with any of
them. Then they called up every boarding house in
town and got no better results there. As Wilks grumbled on the way home, it was like hunting ghosts, and
even Fellows was glum.

Back at headquarters they found Hilders playing
cards at the table in the public part of the main room.
They also found further reports. Gorman had put them
on the chief's desk, and Fellows and Wilks went in
there to digest them. The first was from the State Police lab in Hartford. An analysis of the ashes from both
the fireplace and furnace disclosed, among the usual
fuels, the presence of bone ash and charred bits of flesh.
It confirmed the theory that the missing parts of the
body had been burned, but it added nothing to their
scant supply of knowledge.

The next report was from Bridgeport and said in effect that investigation of Jean Sherman's background
cleared her of complicity in the death of the woman.
She had been home all through that month except for
the weekend trip to New York. Further, no attempt
had been made by any man to visit her and she hadn't
reported any phone calls from John Campbell.

The other reports dealt with the hunt for tan, 1957
two-door Ford sedans with dented rear fenders and so
far none had been found to fit the category. "Worser
and worser," growled Wilks. "If we don't get some
confirmation of something pretty soon I'm going to
start believing this whole thing never happened."

They left the office with long faces and got into their
coats. Hilders, seeing them, swept up his cards and
came over. "I hear you're looking for Campbell's car,
Chief."

Fellows said, "That much you can print."

"I don't want to butt in, but it seems to me you'd
have a better chance of picking up your man if you

broadcast a picture of his face instead of a description of his car."

Fellows, zipping up his jacket, managed a smile. "You got an idea where we can get one?"

"Sure." Hilders was using a different approach on the chief, all eager and co-operative. "You've got three people who've seen him, right?"

"Three?"

"Watly, the delivery boy, and the girl. I know there's a girl and I know you know who she is."

"All right, so?"

"They've described him, right?"

"That's right. And their descriptions tally pretty well, but they'd fit ten million people."

"That's because no one can describe a face. There's a guy on the *Courier*, Don Little, who draws cartoons and stuff. He's the staff artist. Suppose you get the girl and the two men together with him and he can draw what the man looks like with them correcting him."

Fellows rubbed his chin. He said, "Well,—" And then he turned bland eyes on the reporter. "Did you say the girl?"

"Sure. She saw him too, didn't she?"

Fellows shook his head sadly. "Now listen, Hilders, I'm not quite dumb enough to fall into that trap. I told you I'm keeping the girl's identity secret."

Hilders grinned. "You can't blame a guy for trying. All right, you've still got two men who've seen him. I wasn't trying to pitch you a curve. The idea's still valid, isn't it? You get the two men in here to describe him, and I'll get the artist."

Fellows said he'd think about it and then he thanked Hilders and went out with Wilks to their cars. On the way home, he did think about it. At first it was in annoyance because drawing pictures was, to him, in the category with collecting dust. It was grabbing for straws and he wasn't that desperate yet. However, as he ruefully meditated, if reports continued to be as barren as this day's had been, he might get that desperate.

On Sunday morning at the First Congregational Church, Dr. Morse, the minister, mentioned the dead girl in his prayers. Perhaps it was because Fred Fellows was a member, for she was not referred to in any other church. The case did not appear in any newspapers except in the Bridgeport *Courier,* which devoted itself to vice, venery, and victims. Her body lay in a cheap box in the basement of the hospital, waiting final disposition, and the only people who hadn't forgotten her were the policemen of Stockford and the neighboring communities.

Fellows didn't go to church that Sunday. He was uneven in attendance at best, but this time he had the excuse that he could serve God and his fellow man better by putting in the time at headquarters. Sunday was a bad time to get much done since places of business were closed, but he did manage to reach the personnel director of the Graystone Greeting Card Company. The call resulted in the disappointing news that, of the sixty women employees in the place, none with the initials J.S. had left their employ in the two months of the new year. The director promised to check earlier records on Monday to refresh his memory on other ex-employees, but he was sure the information would be negative, for the turnover at the plant was negligible.

"Of course, she could work somewhere else in or around that town," Fellows said to Wilks, but his voice wasn't ringing with conviction this morning.

The detective sergeant sighed. "I've heard of murder cases where you don't know the killer, but this is the first one where you don't even know the victim."

"Or," said Fellows, "if it even was a murder."

"Come on. You don't think it was anything else, do you?"

"I'd stake ten years of my life that it's murder, Sid, but if you don't know how the victim died, how do you prove it in court?"

"You find the guy and hammer at him until he contradicts himself and confesses."

At a little after eleven, Fellows got a call from New York and took it in his office. At quarter past, John Hilders came into headquarters with a copy of the Sunday *Courier* under his arm. He spread it on the counter for Wilks and Unger to see. "I'm owed all the favors I want," he said. "See? I didn't mention any girl in the story."

"You got a particular place you want me to kiss you?" Wilks asked, scanning the paper.

"Where's Fellows?"

"In his office on the telephone."

"Who's he calling?"

"New York's calling him."

Fellows opened the door and came out then. He didn't look happy. "Two people named John Campbell checked in at New York hotels Friday, neither of them Friday night or early Saturday morning. Neither of them is the man we want. They've been cleared."

Wilks said, "Don't look so sad. You said yourself he probably wouldn't use that name."

"I said *maybe* he wouldn't. And another thing. I

called Hartford. Watly and Andy were up there all afternoon yesterday going through their rogue's gallery. They couldn't identify a single face."

"The guy doesn't have a record?"

"If he does, it's not in this state." The chief shook his head. "We're looking, but we're always looking in the wrong places. It's like he's outsmarting us everywhere we turn."

"He's not trying to outsmart us. He's probably running scared."

"It's even worse if he's outsmarting us without even trying." Fellows picked up the *Courier* and glanced at the front-page article. Hilders said, "See? Didn't I treat you right, Fred? You owe me the works."

At the unpermitted familiarity, Fellows's manner turned cool. He said, "You'll get your breaks, Hilders."

"How about letting me look over the murder house?"

"I told you I've got nothing to say about it."

"A phone call to Restlin would let me in. He'd do it for you."

Fellows turned to look at him. "What do you want to see it for?"

"Firsthand report. I want the layout and I want pictures. They should have been in today's paper. You see the rag I write for. My editor plays up the seamy side of everything." He smiled a little. "Besides, well, I'm only an amateur, of course, but covering murders and stuff is my beat and you get some experience. I might be able to come up with a fresh approach."

Fellows said, "Sid, he's after your job."

Hilders said, "Well, I'm not a dummy, you know."

"All right, we'll see. By the way, what's the name of that artist you were telling me about—the one who's on your paper?"

"Don Little."

"Want to give him a call? I think maybe we'll take your advice."

"Now? You wouldn't be able to get him today."

"Why not?"

"He's off. I wouldn't know how to get in touch with him."

"You just said you were a detective. Let's see you detect."

Hilders wet his lips and put his hand on the desk phone. "I talked to him about it last night. He'll expect to be paid."

Fellows said, "On our budget?" His eyes narrowed. "What's he want?"

"Fifty bucks."

Fellows stared at the reporter for a moment in real surprise. Then he moved the phone away. "Sid," he said. "We're in the wrong business. We should've studied our drawing lessons harder in school."

"I tried to tell him," Hilders said. "The guy wouldn't listen. He wants to make a buck."

The chief said, "We got any artists in this town, Sid?"

"Sure. Out in the sticks. I can name you two or three New York illustrators."

"They'd probably want a thousand bucks."

"We can try them. I'll bet Henry Whitlock would do it for nothing."

"I wouldn't have the nerve to ask a guy like him to. No. I've got a better idea. I'm going to call up the art teacher at the high school and find out who her best pupil is. I have a feeling an eager kid like that might turn out a better job. I don't mean it'd be as good art work, but it might be a better likeness."

If all of Fellows's previous efforts had been coming to naught, at least in this instance things went his way. At two o'clock that afternoon, Shirley Whitlock, a dark-haired, attractive sixteen-year-old senior at Stockford High, recommended by her teacher as the outstanding artist in the school, came into headquarters with a sketch pad under her arm and a paper bag of drawing utensils in her hand. Wilks was there to greet her and take her into Fellows's office, where the chief sat at his desk making conversation with Raymond Watly and Andy Palekowski. After the introductions, the chief sat Shirley at the table and said, "Now do you understand what we want you to do?"

"I think so, sir."

"You try to draw a picture of a man the way they tell you to. We want to see if we can't get some kind of a likeness."

"Yes, sir." She tilted the pad against herself and the table and laid an eraser and several extra sticks of charcoal within easy reach. "How should I start?"

Watly said, "I don't know. Why don't you start drawing a head and then we can make corrections." He looked at Andy as the girl sketched an oval quickly. "What do you think? You saw him after I did. Narrower face than that?"

Andy agreed and the girl made changes. It went on like that. Neither man could be sure of the placement of the eyes, whether the forehead was wide or narrow. They let her go ahead.

Fellows and Wilks went out of the office, leaving the door open. The chief could sense the pressure his presence exerted on the trio, on the girl trying to draw with him looking over her shoulder, on the men, worried about their own uncertainty. Wilks said, "Where's that reporter at a time like this? He's missing the only decent news we've had all weekend."

Fellows shrugged. "If he wants to look over the house, let him."

"He's not going to find anything. It's been cleaned up except for the plumbers replacing the pipes."

"It makes him happy. What's the harm?"

Wilks looked sidewise at the chief. "You're big-hearted today. Don't tell me you're falling for that line he threw out about being an amateur sleuth. You do that and you're in a bad way."

Fellows shook his head sadly. "When I turn to running charcoal pictures in the papers, drawn by high school students, of a man as described by two other men who've seen him once in their lives, several weeks before, I'm in a bad way. It's like chasing after every filling-station owner or telling the highway patrols to watch for a tan Ford, or telling other police departments to check on half a dozen guys because they once worked for a hardware factory in Pennsylvania. Face it, Sid. This whole case is in a bad way."

"That's all right. That's police procedure. Track down every clue. But letting some newspaper reporter examine the scene of the crime for new theories, that's admitting failure."

Fellows laughed. "You remind me of the guy who committed suicide when adding machines came out. He couldn't stand having those contraptions beat him. I'm not looking for new theories, but let him have his fun. There's nothing to lose. You've got to understand, Sid. I'm using every resource I can lay my hands on. Hilders is no symbol of anything. He's a resource. Of course he's a faint one, but you never can tell."

He paused briefly, listening to the sounds of discussion emanating from his office. They weren't encouraging sounds, for the men, though dissatisfied with the progress of the drawing, weren't able to suggest effective changes. "The newspapers," Fellows said, turning back to Wilks, "are another resource. We'll run that picture in the papers and hope. And we'll keep publicizing the fact the trunk came from Townsend. One of those two things might do us some good."

At three o'clock a round of coffee was sent out for, and Fellows had the girl and the two men take a break. The girl was close to tears. She had produced a charcoal outline of a face and it was done with a sure and practiced hand, but she was unhappy. "I can't make it come out right, Mr. Fellows."

Watly patted the girl affectionately on the shoulder. "It's not your fault, Shirley." He said to the chief, "I think I'd know him if I saw him, but you pin me down whether his nose was short or long and I can't tell you. I have an impression of his looks, but it's"—he gestured with his hands—"sort of an over-all picture. I can tell her if the picture's wrong, but I can't tell her where it's wrong."

Andy said, "I'd know him, Mr. Fellows. You put him in a line-up, and I'll pick him out. But it's like what Mr. Watly says. I don't know nothing about art. I never drew a picture in my life. This thing looks a little like the guy but not an awful lot and I don't know what she ought to do with it."

"I should throw it away," she complained.

"I wouldn't do that," Fellows told her. "But maybe you could help them out a little by making changes here and there. Experiment and maybe by accident you'll put it together."

The girl said she felt useless, but she tried, and Fellows and Wilks left them together awhile longer.

The picture that finally developed was a pretty good charcoal sketch of a dark-haired man, a little younger looking, perhaps, than thirty-five, with a slender, not unpleasant face. Artistically it was commendable, but the three creators of it weren't well satisfied. Shirley Whitlock was glum and dispirited. Watly shrugged about it and said it might bear some resemblance, but he wasn't willing to commit himself. Andy was a little more optimistic. "It don't look too much like the guy," he said, "but I don't know. There's something about it. I could maybe recognize him from it."

Fellows saw them off with his thanks and put the picture, slightly yellowed by the application of a fixative, on the counter for Wilks and Sergeant Unger to study. "Look like anybody you know?" The two men shook their heads. "Not around here," Unger said.

Wilks handed back the picture. "I think it's going to be a bust, Fred. You really want to give it to the papers?"

"Like Hilders and the house. What's to lose?"

It snowed on Monday the second of March. The first flakes fell at five in the morning and by eight o'clock, there was an inch on the ground, the sky was slate and dark and the weather cold and clammy. It was a dull and depressing start of a new week, but Chief of Police Fred Fellows had hopes. The regional morning papers were publicizing the case again, putting it back on the front pages. Shirley Whitlock's charcoal sketch was given a prominent position in the Stamford editions and the fact that the dead girl's steamer trunk was shipped from Townsend by a man and girl in a pick-up truck got all the play the chief had asked for. People in Townsend read the Stamford papers since they had none of their own and he hoped that before the morning was out there would be a call.

It was this morning too that the report from the Motor Vehicle Department arrived. Of the 873,000 passenger cars registered in the state, 43,000 were 1957 Fords and well over two thousand were tan, two-door sedans.

The information, too lengthy to come over the teletype, arrived by registered mail and when Wilks pulled out the sheaf of papers with names and addresses, he took them in to Fellows and tossed them on his desk and said, "I quit."

Fellows, poring over the roster with an eye to sending more men on the filling-station detail, picked up the lists and tilted his chair back. "What's the matter, Sid?"

"Look at those addresses. Read the letter—873,000 cars in a population of two million. Over two thousand of them match the one we're after. Why couldn't Campbell own a Cord or something? Do you know how long it'll take to check every one of these people?"

"Not long enough for Campbell to die of old age, Sid." He sorted through the thick mess of papers on his desk, hunting until he came up with the Erie police report, the names of the six former employees of Gary Hardware who lived in the area. Then he went through the alphabetical list of Ford owners. At the third Connecticut name he whistled. "Richard Lester at 440 Fair Street, Stamford, owns one of our cars. What do you know about that?"

"Stamford?" Wilks sat down beside him.

"Richard Lester. He worked for Gary Hardware, so he knows about Campbell, he drives the tan Ford, and he lives in Stamford." He finished the sorting and said, "He's the only one, but that's better than I would have thought."

"And the next question," Wilks added, beginning to grin, "is did he know a girl with the initials J.S. I think we're onto something."

"Yeah, but don't let it go to your head. It proves nothing."

"But at least it's a place to look. We haven't even had that before." He got up. "You want me to go down there?"

"I'll send Ed down. The Stamford police are investigating him, but we'll see what Ed can dig up. I want you to go back to Townsend and work on the girl's angle."

"Ed gets all the fun."

"I know it, but you're the better detective. You get the harder job. Try to locate that girl, Sid. And keep in touch by phone in case someone calls in about her."

Ed Lewis was summoned and dispatched in his own car. "It doesn't matter if Lester's got a bent fender or not," Fellows told him. "And if he's not clean, bring him back and we'll show him to Watly or that grocer boy."

Lewis went off eagerly and Wilks went, a little less eagerly, on his assignment in Townsend. His was the harder job, all right, and he didn't have many ideas how to tackle it.

Sidney Wilks was the first to call back. "I tried the employment agency here," he told Fellows. "No luck and no ideas."

"Try the contractors in town. Concentrate on the truck."

"I don't suppose there've been any calls."

"Not about the girl, but there've been three about the picture we ran. They're being checked out now."

John Hilders came in around noon, shaking off snow. "Any news?"

"Not yet. Where'd you disappear to yesterday?"

"I looked over the house and had one of the photographers out. I got enough for a big spread." He grinned. "You miss me?"

"Yeah. I thought you'd come up with a big new theory."

"Give me time." He observed Unger reading from a sheaf of papers, making notations. "What's he doing?"

"That's a list of all owners of tan Fords, the kind Campbell drives. He's noting the ones who live anywhere around this area."

Hilders got out his notebook. "You going to check them all?"

"We're after a guy who drives a tan Ford. What do you think?"

"And I can print it?"

"We're taking the wraps off that angle. You can print it."

Ed Lewis called in at two o'clock. "Richard Lester has a tan Ford, all right, and he used to work for the Gary Hardware Company, Chief, but he doesn't fit the description. He's got sandy hair."

Fellows said slowly, "How old is he?"

"Thirty-eight, and he's about the right build and height, but he's got reddish brown hair."

"Does he look anything like the picture?"

"Look, Chief. I'm telling you. He's not the right guy."

"Does he look like the picture, Ed? I'm asking you."

"Well, some people might see some kind of a resemblance. Personally, I don't."

"What have the Stamford police got on him?"

"They questioned him. He's married, four children, works in the shirt factory here. No dents in his fenders."

"What was he doing nights last month?"

"Staying home."

"Who says so?"

"He does."

"And you're going to take his word for it?"

"Chief, this guy—"

"Has sandy hair. Ed, anybody who can change his name can change the color of his hair. This is the closest thing to a clue we've had yet and I want it checked out. I want proof he's not the right man and if you can't get it, I want him brought in for questioning. Try to get a photograph of him or something we can show Watly or the kid."

As the afternoon passed, Fellows grew restless. Wilks called in twice more reporting no luck and two more phone calls came in about men who resembled the picture in the paper, but none came from anyone who knew of a trunk being sent from Townsend. The picture had now brought in a total of five calls, but not one of the names mentioned could be found on the list of tan Ford owners. Despite this, Fellows had two men busy following up the leads, going out to question the men and make inquiries of their neighbors.

Late in the afternoon, Town Prosecutor Leonard Merrill dropped in from his office upstairs. He listened to Fellows's report of no success with ill-concealed annoyance. He said, "It looks bad for the town, Fellows, when a man can commit murder and get away with it."

"Who said he's going to get away with it?"

"That's what he's doing, isn't it?"

"So far, Len. Only so far."

"You haven't learned a damned thing since the inquest, have you?"

"We've found out a few people it couldn't be. I don't suppose you'd call that learning anything."

"No, I wouldn't."

Fellows sighed. He said, "Wheels are grinding. I guess that's about all I can say."

"The wheels aren't making any noise. People in this town are thinking you're sitting on your hands."

"You been out taking a poll or something?"

"This isn't something to joke about."

"I'm not joking. I'm just reminded of this guy who had a BB gun he liked to play with. So one day he fired a shot into the ceiling and the whole ceiling fell in on him. At the hospital, one of the doctors asked him why he did it and he said he didn't think the ceiling would fall in, he'd been shooting BBs into it for three years and it never happened before."

Merrill said, "What are you telling me a thing like that for?"

"I'm just saying, you don't want to be like that guy with the BB gun, Len. Sure, the wheels grinding don't make much noise and you wouldn't hardly know anything was happening. But you just wait and one of

these days the ceiling's going to fall down and it's going to land right on our boy."

"It'd better be one of these days soon," Merrill said
irritably, and went out.

Shortly after Merrill had gone, Ed Lewis returned
looking gloomier than the town prosecutor. "I've got
the proof," he told Fellows.

"On that guy Richard Lester?"

"That's right. Richard Lester, who works in the shirt
factory. In the first place, he's been putting in overtime
for the past couple of months. This, I found out at the
factory itself. He doesn't get through until six o'clock."

"Meaning," asked Fellows, "that he couldn't have
been at the murder house at five-thirty."

"That's about it. And I talked to his neighbors. They
back up the story he's home nearly every night. In fact,
on three evenings, he was with one of them. You want
the dates?"

Fellows sighed. "I guess you can skip the dates."

"And the weekend that Campbell was supposed to
be in New York, this guy was home. He and his wife
went to a movie with a neighbor couple. That's Saturday before last. You want more?"

"You can keep the rest. He's alibied."

"I told you that earlier."

Fellows said, "Now there's no point in both of us losing our tempers. You can't afford it with me and I
can't afford it for myself. It's one more lead down the
drain, that's all. Go home, Ed. Take your shoes off and
have a beer."

Lewis managed a dry smile. "All right, Chief.
Those're the best orders I've heard since the body was
found."

Fellows took himself in hand after the plainclothesman left and pored over the reports, arguing that pa-
tience was the quality that would eventually break the
case. A certain percentage of leads in all cases were

false and it was to be expected. He'd had enough experience to know that fact, but the disgruntling thing about this particular affair was that all the false leads seemed to be coming at the beginning. He was ready for something more substantial.

The something substantial didn't come from Sergeant Wilks, however. When he returned, Fellows was drinking coffee in the office and Wilks said, "I can tell how tough a case is, Fred, by the coffee you drink."

"I didn't have any lunch."

"You should eat. You'll make yourself sick."

"Never mind about me. What's your report?"

Wilks told him the bad news. He'd checked all the builders in Townsend and questioned everyone connected with them but no one would admit knowing anything about depositing a trunk at the station.

"Any of those guys look like the picture?"

"Not even one. Not even close."

"And nobody's left one of those places recently, nobody who might have used the name Campbell?"

"Give up, will you? Nobody's left, period."

At seven-thirty that evening, while Chief Fellows was eating dinner, the phone rang. His oldest boy, Larry, answered and came back. "It's for you, Dad."

Fellows put down his napkin and went into the bedroom to the telephone table between the closet doors. "Fellows."

"Chief? This is Harris." The patrolman's voice had timbre in it, a suppressed excitement Fellows could sense. "I'm in Stamford," Harris went on. "I've been checking filling stations, trying to finish up now, so I won't have to come back tomorrow. I found a guy who services a tan Ford with a bent rear fender. I showed him the picture. He thinks it might be the same man."

"He know him?"

"He says his name is Clyde Burchard, lives at 62 West Hartford Street. I could go talk to him if you want. He's home right now. Maybe you've got another idea."

"No. Don't do that." Fellows picked up a pencil and scribbled the address. "Go to the Stamford police. Tell them what we've got. Tell them I'm coming down. Ask them to send somebody with you. Stake out the house, but don't tip the guy off and don't touch him unless he tries to leave."

"Yes, sir."

Fellows hung up and immediately dialed another number. "Sid? Fred. We may have a break. Call up that kid Andy, or Watly, or both. Tell them we want them to take a ride down to Stamford with us right away. I'll be by for you in about eight minutes."

Wilks didn't bother to ask for details. He said, "Right," and hung up without waiting for a reply.

Fellows came back, crammed a quarter of a potato in his mouth, and picked up the rest of his chop. "I've got to go out," he mumbled with his mouth full. "Want to get my coat, Larry?"

Larry hurried back with it. "Something to do with the murder?"

"Looks like it," Fellows said, letting his son help him into it while he bit pieces of the chop.

"Can I go with you?"

"What do you ask a foolish question like that for?"

"What's foolish about it?"

"You've got homework for one thing."

"But I want to be a policeman. What's homework compared with practical experience?"

"And I want you to get an education, so you won't have to be a policeman."

It was snowing harder than ever when the chief went out and the temperature had dropped way down. Fellows had trouble starting his car, but he got to Wilks's house at twenty minutes of eight. Wilks opened the door and came down his snow-laden steps before Fellows had completely stopped. He climbed in and said, "Get your heater going, will you?"

"It's on now. The engine hasn't warmed up yet. What about the other two?"

"Both out."

"You couldn't get hold of them?"

"No. Just Andy's mother and Watly's wife."

Fellows set the car in motion, plowing into the seething white flakes. "Oh, well, it may be a pipe-dream anyway." He skidded, getting clear of the curb, and headed slowly out, keeping to the middle of the street.

The highway was pretty clear, but it still took them twenty-five minutes to get into Stamford. Fellows related the details on the way. "It sounds good," he admitted, "but I've been a cop too long to go overboard."

Sixty-two West Hartford Street was a large frame house, three stories high, split into separate apartments. It had a wide porch, an uncleared walk, and a globe of light gleaming from the porch roof in front of the doors. Owners of the other houses were out scraping their shovels into the thick carpet of snow, but the five inches that had fallen that day lay in front of 62, trampled, untouched, and freezing.

Fellows pulled up across the street from the house, behind two other cars, and from there could see the numbers 62 and 60 on either side of the door. When he shut off his motor and lights, three men got out of the car ahead and came to the chief's window. One was Harris, wearing his patrolman's uniform with the earflaps turned down from his cap, swirling clouds coming from his nose and mouth. He introduced the other two as Captain McGarrity and Detective Lieutenant Paulus of the Stamford police. "Burchard's in there," he said. "His car's in the yard in back. Tan Ford, 1957, two doors, bent fender."

Captain McGarrity said, "We're backing you up, Chief. Whatever you want to do."

"Good. I don't know what we've got, but it sounds hot."

Harris said, "His apartment is 2C. He doesn't know he's being watched."

"All right. We'll go in and talk to him. The five of us." Fellows opened his door and got out into the deep snow, Wilks sliding after. Together they crossed the street and mounted the porch. The outer door was locked, but the name "Burchard" was under the top of three bells in the frame below the "62." Fellows pressed the bell and waited.

He had to press it again and then, after a minute, a figure in dark trousers and shirt sleeves was visible through the inside curtains coming down the front staircase. The figure pulled open the inner door and stepped into the vestibule. A perplexed frown crossed his face at the sight of a policeman in uniform with four other men in coats, caps, and hats beside him. He hesitated a moment and opened the door.

"Clyde Burchard?" the chief asked.

"That's right." The man did somewhat resemble the drawing Shirley Whitlock had made. He was somewhere in his thirties, an inch or two under six feet, but of a slender build that made him look taller.

"We're police officers," Fellows told him, pulling his badge from his pocket. "We'd like to ask you a few questions."

Burchard's scowl remained, but he seemed a little less perplexed. "About what?"

"We'd rather ask them in your apartment if you don't mind."

Burchard apparently did mind, but there was little he could do about it. He turned and led the five men up the stairs and down a hall to an open door near the rear. The apartment consisted of a small living room with a smaller bedroom and bath. The living room was furnished in the kind of furniture landlords leave in what they call "furnished" rooms. There was a three quarter bed which served as a couch, a large cabinet radio of ancient vintage, two battered easy chairs, a bookcase against one wall, and a table with a hotplate and coffeepot on it in a corner by one of the two windows. There were curtains on the windows, but they were as drab as the wallpaper, a print of faded figures. Shades were at half mast, and the windows looked into the shaded windows of the next house, fifteen feet away.

Burchard, with his shirt open and slippers on his feet, closed the door behind them and tucked his hands inside his belt at the rear. "Well, what is it?"

Fellows and the captain sat down on the comfortable Hollywood bed, Wilks and the other detective took a look into the rest of the rooms. Harris stood with his back against the door. "We don't like having to disturb you like this," Fellows said, "but we have our job to do."

"All right," Burchard said a little testily. "You're disturbing me. What's the job?"

Fellows put his cap on the couch beside him and scratched his head. "You read anything about that body that was found in Stockford last Thursday?"

Burchard's eyes flickered a little. He said, "No."

"Highland Road was the address. It was a woman. She was in the cellar in a trunk. You know the place?"

"No. Certainly not. What's this got to do with me?"

"We don't know yet, Mr. Burchard. That's why we wanted to ask you some questions. You own that tan Ford in back?"

"Yes, that's my car. What about it?"

"The fellow who lived in that house had a car like it."

"What?" Burchard exhaled and a good deal of the strength went out of his legs. He sat down in one of the chairs.

"You happen to have rented that house by any chance?"

"No," he breathed. "And anybody who says I did is a liar."

Wilks reappeared in the bedroom doorway. He said, "C'mere a minute, Fred."

Fellows and Captain McGarrity both got up and followed him into the bedroom. Burchard swallowed, but

didn't try to leave his chair. There was only room for
a bed, a bureau, and a night table in the room's
cramped confines, and Paulus had to leave to let the
chief in. Fellows stepped past, looked around, and
arched his brows. There were a dozen or more pictures
of girls in the room, varying in size from snapshots to
eight by ten studio portraits and no two were of the
same person.

Fellows nodded with thoughtful interest, then he
moved closer and made a careful examination of all the
brunettes, of which there were eight. McGarrity said,
"You think one of them might be the girl?"

"Wouldn't be surprised, Captain," Fellows murmured. "This fellow gets around. I wouldn't be surprised at all." He pursed his lips, studying first one,
then another. "Too young, that one. Also that one. This
one isn't bosomy enough. This one, possibly. Maybe
this—" He fell silent going over the rest. In the other
room Burchard could be heard saying to Paulus, "What
is it? What are they doing?" He was alarmed and he
couldn't keep the fact out of his voice. The chair
creaked, and Paulus said abruptly, "You just stay
where you are, Burchard. They don't want to be dis-
turbed."

"But they've got no right—"

Fellows selected three of the pictures and sorted
through them one after the other. "You take a girl's
head off," he muttered, "and there isn't much you can
tell about her." He went back to the living room again,
taking the three questionable photographs with him,
and sat on the couch. McGarrity joined him, looking
grim. Wilks and Paulus stood by the bedroom door.

The photographs were in plain sight, and Burchard
kept eyeing them. Fellows said, "Now, Mr. Burchard.
What was it you said about that house?"

Burchard wet his lips. "I said I don't know anything
about it."

"Are you married, Mr. Burchard?"

There was a little shriek in his voice as he gestured. "Do I look married?"

"That's not an answer, Mr. Burchard."

"No, I'm not married!"

"That's quite a harem in your bedroom."

"All right, I go out with girls. Is that a crime?"

"Not when Congress last reconvened, Mr. Burchard. You like girls quite a lot, don't you?"

"I'm not a homo, if that's what you mean."

"That's not an answer."

"Yes, I like girls. What's that supposed to prove?"

"How long have you lived here?"

"Eighteen months."

"And what's your occupation, Mr. Burchard?"

"I sell vacuum cleaners."

Fellows had had a faint hope he might mention hardware. This answer was even better. It was ten times better. It went a long way to explain that strange event of Mr. Campbell bringing home a vacuum cleaner when the house already had one. He looked at Wilks, and the sergeant's answering look caused perspiration to break out on Burchard's face. He said a little desperately, "Is that supposed to be against the law too?"

Fellows turned to him. "I think, Mr. Burchard, you'd better recognize you're in something of a jam, here. The house where we found the dead girl was rented by a man called John Campbell—"

"Mine is Clyde Burchard."

"Called John Campbell," the chief repeated. "It wasn't his real name, of course. His real name could be anything, including Clyde Burchard."

"I never rented any such house."

"Do you have any way to prove that?"

"What do you mean prove it? You can't prove I did."

"That remains to be seen." Fellows reached out to

hand Burchard one of the pictures. "Want to tell us this girl's name?"

He looked at the proffered photograph without taking it. "No. Why should I?"

"Why shouldn't you?" Fellows kept the picture at arm's length.

Burchard looked away from it, turning to the chief. "Because it's none of your business. What right have you got coming in here asking me a lot of questions? I haven't done anything."

"We can't just take your word on that, I'm afraid." Fellows replaced that picture and held out another. "Who's this girl?"

"I'm not going to tell you. I said that before."

Fellows gave up with a sigh. "Can you tell us what you did last weekend? The one before this one?"

"Why?"

"Because everything you've told us so far goes against your claim you know nothing about this. If you're innocent, you ought to have some way of convincing us."

He said, "I was away that weekend."

"Where did you go?"

"I went to New York."

"How did you get there?"

"I took the train."

"What train?"

"I got one around six o'clock. It's the one I usually take."

"You go to New York every weekend?"

"Nearly every weekend."

"Why?"

"What do you think I'm going to do? Stay here?"

"You're not answering my question, Mr. Burchard."

"To have some fun, of course."

"Somebody special you go to see in New York?"

"Not necessarily."

"Want to tell me her name?"

"No, I don't. I said I'm not giving out names. But I can tell you one thing. If you try to prove I did anything that weekend, I can bring her in here and make a liar out of you."

"See anybody you knew on the train, Mr. Burchard? Did you meet anybody on the train? Someone who could kind of back up your story?"

"No."

"You didn't sit next to a girl, maybe, and chew the fat with her?"

"No."

Fellows regarded the man thoughtfully for a moment. Then he said, "Have you ever been in jail, Mr. Burchard?"

Burchard looked grim, but he didn't answer.

"We can find out," Fellows reminded him. "You'd be better off telling us yourself."

The man said sullenly, "Once. I served part of a two-year sentence."

"What for?"

"A girl told me she was eighteen. Her parents proved she wasn't."

Fellows accepted that and tried another tack. He asked questions about the others in the house, who the landlord was, when and how he sold the vacuum cleaners. Burchard said he knew little of the other people in the house, that he seldom saw them. He said the landlord was a landlady who lived on the first floor on the opposite side. He sold vacuum cleaners during the day and did pretty well at it.

"Pretty well?" Fellows asked and glanced around the apartment. "But you live here? What's the rent?"

"Forty a month. But I only sleep here. I'm not going to waste my money on a place to flop."

As for his technique in selling, he said he'd pick a neighborhood and hit all the houses. Blind calls, he described them, and he was successful at it. "It's a percentage," he explained nervously. "If you know how to sell, and you pick the right neighborhood, one that's not too classy, you can figure on so many calls to make a sale. So it's just a question of putting in the time." Burchard lit a cigarette and his hands were shaking.

Fellows said, "A man in your work can take off all the time he wants, I guess."

"You can, but you don't make any money doing it. And beyond a certain point the company will give you the fish eye."

Fellows said to Wilks, "Sid, while we're talking here, why don't you run down and see the landlady. We've got time."

Wilks nodded and went out. Burchard watched him and took quick puffs on his cigarette. "Listen, I haven't done anything. I don't know anything about any woman in Stockford."

"You canvass houses in Townsend when you're trying to sell vacuum cleaners?"

"I go all over this area."

"How about showing us your records?"

He jumped a little. "Records? What records?"

"Of your calls. You must keep a record, Burchard."

"It's in my head. I don't write that stuff down."

The chief said, with sudden impatience, "Listen, Burchard, I want to know who you called on in Townsend. The more you stall, the deeper in you get. Now tell me."

He put a hand to his forehead. "I can't remember. You've got me all mixed up."

Fellows got up and looked around. There were no places for papers in the living room and he returned to the bedroom, opening drawers in the bureau. He didn't have to go beyond the top ones. Scattered papers half filled the right-hand drawer and he went through them slowly. Burchard watched through the door from his chair. He swallowed several times, but the presence of the other officers kept him silent.

The only informative papers were order-form duplicates that contained names and addresses of sales made. Fellows read every one. Most were in the Stamford area, but there were four in Townsend, one in Ashmun, and three in Stockford, as well as a scattering from other surrounding towns. Fellows copied the Townsend ones and put the papers back.

"All right," he said, rejoining him. "Maybe tomorrow you can show us all the places you've been to in Townsend, all the calls you made there."

"I can't. I'll be on the road."

Fellows shook his head at McGarrity, and the captain snapped, "Not tomorrow, Burchard. We're holding you."

"Holding me? For what?"

Fellows said, "Suspicion of murder."

Burchard came out of the chair like a shot, and McGarrity and Paulus converged on him. "You can't," Burchard yelped. "You—you've got nothing to hold me for. I haven't done anything. I'm innocent."

Fellows stood up too. "That may be, Mr. Burchard, but we're not convinced of it. Not by quite a bit."

"You think I killed that woman in Stockford? You're crazy. I've never even been to Stockford."

"You sold three vacuum cleaners there, Burchard. You've been there all right, and we don't think making calls is all you did." Fellows raised a hand as Burchard tried to protest. "Now don't tell me again how innocent you are. Just get your coat and your shaving things, if you want, and come along with us."

Burchard said, "You càn't do this," but he knew they could. He put on a tie in the bedroom with Fellows and McGarrity standing in the door. He went into the bathroom, with the chief following, got his shaving kit while mumbling that he was going to call a lawyer and sue for false arrest. He took a jacket out of the closet and put that on, then got into a dark winter overcoat and scarf, taking a dark brown hat from the shelf.

When he stepped away, Fellows took a look into the closet himself. A tan overcoat was also there, of lighter weight, and a gray spring topcoat. There were two other hats and half a dozen suits of varying shades.

Fellows closed the closet and followed Burchard into the living room where Harris opened the door. The five of them went down the stairs and stopped for Wilks, who was inside the front apartment door in the hall talking to the landlady.

Outside, at the car, Wilks put handcuffs on the man while Fellows had a brief conference with McGarrity. "He's our pigeon," Fellows said, coming back. "McGarrity's letting us take him."

They put Burchard in the rear seat, guarded by Wilks, and drove back to Stockford in silence, Harris following in his own car.

Monday, 10:30 P.M.— **16**
Tuesday, 12:45 A.M.

Clyde Burchard was put in a cell in the block behind the police waiting room at ten-thirty that evening. Wilks and Harris took the contents of his pockets, his wrist watch, belt, garters, and shoelaces, and gave him a receipt while Fellows called up the grocer boy again.

When Wilks returned from the cell block, Fellows was sitting in his chair at his desk, tilting back with his arms on the armrests, his eyes closed. He opened them when Wilks came in to report things under control.

"I gather the landlady didn't clear him," Fellows said.

Wilks pulled up another chair. "She says she doesn't know what her tenants do. Most of the time she doesn't know whether they're in or not."

"Or if they've got girls in?"

"I asked her about that. She didn't know and didn't seem to care. As long as she gets the rent and there's no noise and nothing gets damaged, her tenants can do as they like."

Fellows said, "He wears good clothes, and he fits the description." He sat up. "I got hold of that kid, Andy. He's coming right down."

"You going to let him identify him tonight?"

"Why not? If we're wrong, I don't want to keep the guy in jail. If we're right, the sooner we know it the better."

Andy arrived ten minutes later, coming through the side door in a too thin jacket and no gloves. Wilks, Fellows, and Sergeant Gorman were at the main table drinking coffee, and the young lad pulled off his cap and said, "I'm here, Chief. What is it you want me to do?"

Fellows produced an extra container of the liquid for the boy, who sat down to it with mixed pleasure and awe. "I only want you for a minute, Andy. Sergeant Wilks and I are going to show you a man we've got in a cell beyond that steel door. I don't want you to say anything while we're in there, but after we leave, I want you to tell me if you've ever seen him before."

"Sure. I get it. Is this the guy?"

"I'm not saying who it is or why we want you to look at him, Andy. When you finish your coffee, just follow us and, remember, don't speak while you're there."

They didn't make the boy hurry, letting him smoke a cigarette over the beverage, and Fellows even tried one of Andy's cigarettes himself, smoking it experimentally, contrasting the effect with chewing. Wilks was a little restless at the chief's lack of speed in settling the issue and Gorman was downright impatient, though he tried hard to conceal it.

Then, when they were all through, the three left Gorman behind, and Wilks slipped back the heavy bolts on the sheet steel cell-block door and pulled it open. The gap revealed a long, dimly lighted hall to a head-high barred window at the end that looked out onto the yard. Six small cells were spaced on the right, each with its worm's-eye barred window, and Burchard was in the farthest one down, the only one occupied.

The three walked down the cement hallway and

stopped in front of his door. Burchard was sitting on his bunk against the side wall, his tieless shirt open, his beltless pants sagging, his laceless shoes on his feet. His jacket was neatly folded on the bunk beside him, for the windows were closed and the steam heat of the building kept the tightly stoppered area overwarm. He was slumped in dejection with his elbows on his knees, and he looked up at their arrival, staring at them dully, without expression.

Fellows said, "Are you comfortable, Mr. Burchard?"

The man answered with a snort. "Mister Burchard!" He spit at the wall. "You come in like the Gestapo and pull a guy out of his house and slap him in jail in the middle of the night and then you think if you act like Emily Post, it's going to be all right."

"I'm doing my job, Mr. Burchard."

"Who's the kid supposed to be?"

"Take a look at him, Mr. Burchard."

Burchard did. He took a long look and thereby gave Andy an equally good look at him. He said, "I looked. Are you happy?"

Fellows and Wilks turned back with Andy, and the youth couldn't completely hide his eagerness. Halfway down the hall he whispered loudly, "It's him. That's the guy."

"All right. Keep it quiet." They went out and bolted the door again. Andy was almost jumping. "He's the man. He's the man at that house, the one with the tan Ford. How'd you find him?"

"You're sure, now? You're absolutely sure?"

"Hell, yes—I mean—sure I'm sure. I'll swear to it on a stack of Bibles. I wouldn't ever forget that man."

"Would you be willing to swear to it in court?"

"Any time! You just let me get into court and I'll swear it any time."

They sent the boy home, and Wilks clapped Fellows on the back. "How about that, Freddie, boy? How about that? You going to call Merrill?"

Sergeant Gorman cocked his head. "Ssh. What's that?"

They listened. Through the steel door came the faint sound of hollering. Fellows went over and pushed back the bolts and he and Wilks returned through the corridor to where Burchard gripped the steel bars and shouted.

"All right," Fellows said. "Quiet down, Burchard. You can talk to a lawyer in the morning."

"Listen," Burchard was saying. "Listen to me. Who was that kid?"

"You don't recognize him?"

"Who was he? I've got a right to know."

Fellows shook his head. "I don't know what rights you do have, Mr. Burchard, you being a prisoner. But I guess we can tell you. He's one of the witnesses we've got who laid eyes on the man called Campbell."

"Is he claiming I'm Campbell?"

"He's swearing to it, if you want to know."

"That's not true. Who is he? Where did he claim he saw me? Where does he get the idea I'm Campbell?"

"He delivered groceries to you, Mr. Burchard. Friday the thirteenth of last month to be exact. At two Highland Road."

Burchard sagged. He said, "Oh, my God."

"And then some, mister. Now you keep quiet in here."

"Listen. Listen, Chief. I want to talk."

They got Ed Lewis in to take down the statement since he was the shorthand man on the force, and when he arrived, they brought Clyde Burchard into the chief's office, seating him at the end of the table there, back by the cabinets. Wilks and Lewis sat opposite each other on either side of the table and the chief, swinging his desk chair around sat at the head. When Lewis was ready, he said, "All right, Mr. Burchard. You want to make a statement."

Burchard swallowed. "I do." He wet his lips. "First

off, I want to say I'm innocent. I want to get that down on the record."

"All right. Mr. Lewis has that down. I hope you have more than that."

Burchard nodded. He said, "I guess some of the things I told you back at my place weren't exactly the truth." No one answered him. He looked into sets of steadily staring eyes. "All right. I—you came at me so fast I—" He had his jacket on now and slapped the pockets. "In that envelope you've got with all my things there's a notebook. I want you to look at it."

Fellows left without a word and came back with the sealed manila envelope Gorman had locked in the safe. He broke it open, dumped the contents.

"That's it," Burchard said, pointing to a worn brown dime-store pocket notebook.

Fellows didn't pick it up right away. "What is it?"

"My record book. I told you I didn't have one, but I did. That's a complete list of my calls, addresses of all the houses."

Fellows still didn't touch it. "What's that mean to us?"

"Read what it says for Friday the thirteenth."

The chief finally picked it up and thumbed through the pages, pausing to read with a blank face. He put it down open in front of him and said, "What's this supposed to prove?"

"Don't you see it there? Two Highland Road, Stockton?"

"I saw it. With an asterisk beside it."

"Well, don't you see? I made a call there. That's how the delivery boy saw me. I was there trying to sell the woman a vacuum cleaner."

"And you pay for the groceries and you come out of the house in your shirt sleeves and park your car in the drive? And when you're asked about it you lie and say you never went near the place? Is that what we're supposed to believe?"

"It's the truth."

Fellows bent over the page again. "You told me your method of selling is to saturate a neighborhood. This is the only call you've got anywhere near that neighborhood, Mr. Burchard. Since it's the last entry on that day and there are blank lines after it, I'd guess a more likely explanation is that you wrote that in some other time to cover yourself."

"I can explain all that," Burchard said desperately. "You see that asterisk beside the name? You know what that means?"

"No."

"It means the lady is willing."

Fellows was silent as he turned through the other pages in the book. "I count four other asterisks, Mr. Burchard. Are you trying to tell me those ladies are also willing?"

He nodded. "But please don't let it get in the papers. Those women are married."

Fellows closed the notebook and tossed it onto the desk behind him. "So far, Mr. Burchard, I don't see that you've explained anything."

Burchard spread his hands. "Look, this is what happened. You came in and asked me about that house and that woman and I lied about not knowing her because, hell, I can't go around letting it be known that some of the people I call on don't mind a little play on the side. I've got that sentence on my record and the moment I'm asked about me and some woman, especially some married woman, I'm going to play dumb. That's the whole trouble. Once I said I didn't know her, I was stuck with it. I kept getting in deeper. Well, I don't want to admit anything like this, but what you're pegging me for isn't fooling around, it's murder. You can do what you want to me for making plays, but I'm not getting sent up for knocking off some dame. I'd never do a thing like that."

Fellows said, "I'm still waiting for your explanation."

"I was out making calls, see? So I decide I'll hit that area. I never touched it before and it looked ripe. So the first house I stop at is this number two, corner house. I park in front and get out my demonstrator and lug it up to the stoop. Well, this woman opens the door. She's a nice-looking woman, not beautiful, but good-looking and well built. I don't want you to get the idea, Chief, that I make passes at everyone who opens a door, but a man gets so he can tell when he meets a woman if she'd be interested in a pass. I'm telling you, she was interested. I don't know that I blame her, living out in the sticks alone like that. You tell me she was married. Well, I didn't honestly know that when I met her. In fact, I thought she wasn't married on account of she wasn't wearing any ring. So when she acted friendly-like, really glad to see me, you can't blame me for figuring, O.K., anything she wants, I'll take her up on. This girl, I want to tell you, wasn't any kid. She knew her way around as well as I did. We spoke the same language right from the start and it was obvious what we were talking about wasn't going to be vacuum cleaners.

"Well, she gets out a bottle and I take off my coat and tie and get ready to make myself at home. Now what I mean about her knowing the score is she brings in the liquor and she looks out the window and she says I should move the car. She thinks it would look bad for some salesman's car to be sitting out front of the house for an hour or more. If I put it in the drive, it'll look more like I belong there. She says, especially, there's a nosey dame across the way who'd be sure to notice the car and start drawing conclusions. So I move the car into the drive and just when I'm getting out, up comes this grocery truck and a guy gets out with a box full of food. I can't see any point in him bringing it in the house and maybe wondering who I am and what it's all about, her and me there alone. You see, I don't know what's what about the place. All I know is the girl's name is Joan—Joan Campbell, she calls herself. I don't know what she's doing there or anything else—meaning whether she's married or lives with her family, or lives there alone, or what, so I don't want to do anything that's going to look out of the way. I pay for the groceries myself, so the kid won't be coming in and I send him on his way and go back inside. She paid me back for them as soon as I came in. I wasn't even buying her anything.

"So anyway, I was there until nearly five o'clock, I guess. Then it's time for me to go and I lug the demonstrator back to the car and take off. O.K. You're wondering why I wasn't making any more calls in that area. Well, do you think I'd call on someone else and then have the neighbors know I'm selling vacuum cleaners? Me, spending an hour and a half with that Joan Campbell? I got a little more respect for women than that. And besides, it was quitting time anyway and besides that, well, who the hell wants to go sell vacuum cleaners after that visit? I'm asking you." He paused and looked around. "Now that's my story and it's the truth."

Fellows sat very still for a good many seconds. He wanted to punch holes in the tale, but he didn't quite know how. The trouble was, it could actually have happened that way. It was a perfectly plausible explanation and there wasn't one loose thread he could seize on. A woman who'd live with a man under an assumed name would be quite capable of an adventure like that, so the Burchard story even took her character into consideration. Finally he said, "You made no attempt to see her again?"

"I starred her name. That was just in case I was in the neighborhood and felt in the mood, but I don't often go back to places."

"And when did you learn she was dead?"

"When you told me tonight, Chief. I swear, that's the first I heard of it."

"It's been in the papers."

"I don't read the papers much. I might have seen it, but I wouldn't have connected it. Honest I wouldn't."

"One of those photographs in your collection a picture of her?"

"Hell no. Those are just pictures I picked up over the years, from high school and the war on. I guess the latest one is five years old."

Wilks asked a few questions then, but his were no more pointed than the chief's. The story was believable and, against their will, they found themselves believing it. One thing, of course, remained. They would show him to Raymond Watly in the morning.

There was one other thing, and Fellows did it that evening after Burchard was returned to his cell. He copied all the Townsend addresses from Burchard's record notebook. It would help break down his story if they found the murder victim had lived at one of them.

"At least," Wilks said as they departed from headquarters late that night, "we can guess the 'J' in her initials stands for 'Joan.' "

Tuesday was mild and almost warm with a bright sun eating up the snow. When Raymond Watly pulled into the yard behind the town hall at quarter after nine, the streets were slushy and the gutters runny. He came down the concrete steps wearing rubbers and an un-buttoned coat, pulled open the basement door, and entered. "The chief wants to see me. I'm Raymond Wat-ly," he explained to Sergeant Unger.

Fellows came out of his office with Wilks, greeted the man, and explained the nature of the situation. They took him down the long corridor past the empty cells to Clyde Burchard. Burchard, reading on his bunk, got up and made a bitter comment, and Watly looked him over carefully. The real estate agent shook his head. "That's not the man, Chief. That's not the John Campbell I met."

They brought Watly back to the main room and he explained that there was a bit of a resemblance, the shape of the face and mouth, but that was as far as it went. They thanked him and he went away again.

Burchard wasn't released immediately, however. Fel-lows wasn't overlooking the possibility of an accom-plice, and he would not be satisfied with Burchard's innocence until the Townsend addresses in his report book had been checked. There were sixteen such listed, and two men had been sent out that morning to investigate each one.

Meanwhile, other activities were taking place. With the hunt for the man in the case at a dead end, the search was redoubled for the woman's identity. A request was sent to the Bureau of Internal Revenue in Hartford for names and addresses of any woman in Townsend, Connecticut with the initials J.S. Three other men were also in Townsend, working with Chief Ramsey, asking questions of shopkeepers and business establishments, trying to find someone who worked for or traded with such people. Fellows had his men pay particular attention to beauty parlors and drug stores.

At noon Daniels and Hogarth, checking out the report book, called in to say that one of the sixteen addresses in the Burchard book had a woman with the initials J.S. living there, but she was the one who answered the door. "None of the others are even close, Chief. One of them was an address he had a star beside, and she gave me a funny look when I mentioned his name. Is that supposed to mean something?"

"Not a thing. I'm not hunting for looks."

"What next, Chief? Do we come back?"

"Stay there. See Ramsey and find out where our other men are, then you two go help them."

At half past twelve, Clyde Burchard was given his lunch and then brought to the chief's office. "We're going to let you go," Fellows said. "Looks like there's a good chance you're telling the truth."

Burchard didn't castigate the chief for inconveniencing him, for wrecking half a day's selling, or threaten suit against the town of Stockford. Thirteen hours in a cell with a murder charge hanging over his head had changed his outlook. All he could feel was a relief so great he could hardly stand. "Thanks," he said weakly.

And then, because he felt he had to say something else, "I told you I was innocent."

"Right now it looks that way. But I wouldn't leave town, Burchard. We'd take a different view of things if you left town."

"No. I won't."

"Sit down. Take a chair."

Burchard sat gratefully and Fellows swiveled around. "Here's your report book, Burchard. As for your other activities, I'd lay off if I were you. I'm not going to tell you what I think of a man who seduces other men's wives. I am going to tell you you've got one conviction on a morals charge and if you get another, you're in real trouble. A copy of your statement is going to the Stamford police, and they're going to keep an eye on you. When you make a call, you'd better sell vacuum cleaners and nothing else."

"Yes, sir."

Fellows took out his chewing tobacco and changed the tone of the conversation. "Now there are a few more questions I want to ask you about that girl who called herself Joan Campbell. She wear any rings or other jewelry?"

"She had a wrist watch."

"What kind?"

"I don't know, sir. I've never bought that kind of a present for a girl in my life."

"Describe it."

"It was small, round, and gold, with a black sort of string strap."

Fellows noted that down. "Earrings?"

"No, sir."

"What were her teeth like? Any missing?"

"If there were, it wasn't where they showed at all."

"What kind of a personality did she have? In short, what was she like?"

"I didn't know her very long."

"I realize you spent most of the time in bed with her, but she did talk, she did have a character to go with the body. You must have noticed something about her. Was she easygoing, or neurotic, was she a nymphomaniac, was she frustrated, was she eager or merely permissive? When she did talk, what was it about?"

Burchard licked his lips. "She was interested, but she didn't attack me. She wasn't a nympho. I'd guess she was maybe frustrated. As for what we talked about, I don't remember. We didn't talk much."

That was all Fellows could get from him, and he let him go, feeling as much relief at Burchard's departure as Burchard himself. "I'm no prude," he told Wilks when the detective sergeant came in half an hour later, "but a guy like him makes me want to take a bath."

Wilks said, "It was just a little vacation from the main business. I guess we're up a tree until we get a break. Harris called in. The beauty parlor brainstorm just fell through."

"Well, I've got another brainstorm. I want all pawnshops in the district we've marked out checked for watches brought in after February twentieth. Here's the description of it."

Wilks took that out with him and started the wheels rolling.

Through the afternoon other reports came in, but they were all negative and by the end of that working day, the watch was the only lead still being investigated. Everything else had ended in failure. Druggists and shopkeepers in Townsend had all been questioned, but could give no aid, and the search for the girl had come up against a blank wall.

"I keep thinking more and more that the girl doesn't live there," Wilks said as he sat in Fellows's office looking over the completely fruitless results of five men's work. "We've hit every office and every shop in that town. Where else would she work? About all that's left

are the doctors and dentists, but somehow I don't picture her as a nurse or receptionist."

"But if you're going to send a trunk, Sid, you're going to send it from the nearest station, aren't you?"

"Unless there's some reason we don't know about
why she can't."

"Name one."

Wilks was stymied. He said, "All right. She lives
there. Why don't we turn her up?"

"We aren't asking the right people."

"Name some right people we haven't been asking."

Fellows smiled. He thought for a moment and suddenly snapped his fingers. "I really am stupid."

"What?"

"Dentists. You just mentioned dentists. There's a
possible clue right there." He looked at his watch and
picked up the phone.

"If you're going to try to identify her through her
teeth, Fred, you're forgetting she doesn't have any
head."

"But she'd go to a dentist, wouldn't she?" Fellows
started dialing. "That's one place a person would almost certainly go where she'd be known." He said into
the phone, "Chief Ramsey, please. Fellows calling." To
Wilks he added, "It's not quite five yet. We might
catch a dentist or two before they go home. Hello?
Ramsey? Say, what's the name of your dentist?" He
grinned at the response and said, "I want to know the
dentists in Townsend. How many are there? . . . Well,
give me the name and phone number of yours, will
you?"

He wrote the data on a loose paper amid the thickly
messed desk in front of him. "Norman Sinclair," he told
Wilks, and dialed the number. He caught Dr. Sinclair
about to leave the office and told him the nature of his
business. He wanted the names and phone numbers of
every other dentist in town and the names and ad-

dresses of every woman patient under forty with the initials J.S.

The doctor was reluctant both to part with such information and to go through the files to hunt for it. "How can I be sure you're who you say you are? This is confidential information."

"You call me back when you've got it and reverse charges. Tell the operator you want Stockford Police Headquarters, Doctor. Is that satisfactory?"

"I suppose so."

"Doctor, this is important. This is a murder case and the information may break it for us. We need your help."

The doctor felt impressed, important, and more willing. He agreed to help and even volunteered to notify the other two dentists in town himself since they had offices in the same building. He said they'd call back with the complete list as soon as they had it ready.

It took them half an hour to assemble the information and Fellows spent it going through his own reports, listing the names of all the J.S.'s in Townsend who had been cleared. When the call came in, Fellows pulled over a fresh sheet of paper.

"We count eight such people between us," Dr. Sinclair said. "Do you want just their names and addresses?"

"That and any pertinent information you may have such as if they're married, have children, and the like."

"As follows, then. Mrs. Josephine Stevens, two children—"

"She's not the one. This woman never had a child."

"Judy Sorenson. Eighteen, 113 Edgehill Road."

Fellows didn't bother with that name. "All right, next."

"Joan Simpson, 535 Market Street. That's all I know about her. She's not my patient."

"You said Joan?"

"That's right. Jane Smathers, 169 Eastwood Street. Nothing more on her. Joan Steckle, 74 Williams Street. Mrs. Jessica Smith, 88 Eastwood Street, Mrs. Jennifer Sand—no. She's got children. So has this one." He paused. "I guess that's the list."

"Do you have phone numbers for these people?"

"Yes, you want that?"

Fellows did, and Sinclair read them off. Fellows thanked him and hung up. "Joan Simpson, Jane Smathers, Joan Steckle, and Jessica Smith," he said, and Wilks sat down with him to check off names and addresses against the list of cleared names. A Joan Simpson was found, but her address was different from the one Sinclair had given. "Keep her," Fellows said. "There may be two Joan Simpsons in town." They kept Jane Smathers too, but the other two names belonged to women on the other list who were known to be very much alive.

"Joan and Jane," said Fellows. "Two J.S.'s all our other research failed to turn up." He turned to the phone again. "Let's try Joan first."

The call was answered by a girl's voice, and the chief said, "May I speak to Joan Simpson please?"

There was a moment's silence and then the girl said, "Joan doesn't live here any more."

"When did she leave?"

"She moved out the end of January. Who is this?"

Fellows introduced himself. He said, "May I have your name?"

"Ruth Cary."

"Could you tell me why she left and where she went?"

"She got married. I don't know where they're living. I haven't heard yet."

Fellows said, "This is very important. Will you arrange to be home at eight o'clock this evening? I want to talk to you."

When he hung up, his eyes glowed with a steely light. "Sid," he said, "the ceiling's getting ready to fall in."

The Market Street address was a brick apartment
house three stories high, two wings enclosing a small
court. At a few minutes after eight that night, Wilks
and Fellows crossed the court along a cement walk that
branched to the different entries and entered the main
lobby straight ahead. There, the chief set down the
suitcases he carried and ran his finger down the list of
names and said, "Ruth Cary, 6E." They went out again
to entry six and climbed to the top story to ring the
bell.

Ruth Cary was a pretty redhead in her middle twenties with a pert manner and an interesting way of tilting her head. She looked at the two men and at the
two suitcases and nodded at the introductions. She
closed the door soberly behind them and said of the
suitcases, "Are those Joan's? What's happened?"

Fellows said, "That's what we'd like to find out."
He sat down with Wilks on the couch as Miss Cary
took a chair between the door and a table. She bit her
lip and said, "What did Joan do?"

"You read about the dead woman found in Stockford?"

"I read something about it. I don't know anything

really." She leaned forward a little. "You don't mean it was Joan, do you?"

"That's what we're trying to find out. These suitcases and a green trunk were found in the house. Do you recognize the suitcases?"

Ruth Cary was uncertain. "Joan had a couple of suitcases like those, but I can't remember whether hers had initials. Her trunk was kept in the cellar. She only brought it up when she moved. I don't see how she could be the girl you found. She left town. She got married and moved out West."

"You don't want to identify the suitcases?"

She shook her head. "I can't be sure they're hers."

Fellows lifted the smaller to the cushion beside him and got up to open it. "Maybe you can identify some of her things. Would you care to take a look?"

The girl came over reluctantly, and Fellows lifted the lid. The belongings inside were not neatly folded. They hadn't been when the locksmith had opened the luggage, and the police, when they inventoried the items, were careless in replacing them. Fellows took out some underthings on the top which were store bought and meant nothing. Then came a blouse, a dress, and a sweater. Ruth Cary said tensely, "Those are hers." Then she drew out an item herself. She said, "That's my blouse," and burst into tears.

Fellows helped her back to her chair and she said she was sorry and blew her nose. He repacked the suitcases and met Wilks's eye. Death was a sorry fact at all times, but at last a break had come. At last they knew who was dead. He put the suitcase back on the floor and said solicitously to the girl, "Can I get you a glass of water or something?"

If the blouse made her weep, Fellows's remark brought about an opposite effect. She laughed through her tears and got herself under control. "Why," she asked, "does a man always say something like that—as though water was a miracle cure?" She wiped her eyes and said, "I'll be all right now. It's just—it's such a shock. She lived with us and now she's been murdered."

"Maybe you can help us find out who did it."

She put her handkerchief away. "I want to."

"You said she got married, or she told you she got married. We'd like to know who the man was."

Ruth leaned on her knees and shook her head. "I can't tell you."

"Can't or won't?"

"Can't. I don't have the faintest idea."

"We think he may have been the man who took her trunk to the station in a pick-up truck. That ring any bells?"

She smiled a little at that. "That was Bob Herald. He's Helen's beau—my other roommate. He has a chicken farm and that was his truck."

"We'll want to talk to him."

Ruth said, "He'll be here. Helen's having dinner with him, but when I said you'd called, she said they'd come right back."

Fellows nodded. Then he asked the girl to tell him everything she could about the dead girl. Joan, Ruth related, worked as a secretary for the Fizz-Rite Cola Company. Originally she was in their main office in Bridgeport, but when a branch bottling plant was opened between Townsend and Stamford, she was transferred. This had happened two years before in the fall. Through one of the new girls who'd been hired, she learned of the apartment Ruth and Helen had and that they would not be averse to having an additional roommate to help defray the rent. The two girls, who worked together in the greeting card company, met and talked to Joan and took her on, Joan moving in at the beginning of the previous February. Since Ruth and Helen worked together and had grown up together, and since they were five or six years younger than Joan, they weren't too close to her. "We date a lot, for instance," Ruth said, "and Joan never had any dates at all. At least not at first. But we got along very well. She sort of played mother to us. She wasn't a wallflower, you understand. She was very attractive and I think she had lots of dates in her time, but she was thirty at least and, you know, that's practically death.

"I think her problem was she really wanted to get married. I don't mean she talked about it, but you can tell. Helen and I sometimes tried to get her a date at our place, but we never had any luck. There weren't many people to ask. Most of the men we know are younger than thirty, and the older men are already married. She didn't ask us to, but she was interested in our dates and we knew she wished she had some too.

"And then one day, it was last April or May sometime, she went out herself. She said she was going to the movies, but Helen and I suspected she had a beau. At least she had a kind of glow when she came home like she'd had a date instead of going to the show alone, if you know what I mean. After that, she started going out now and then. It wasn't every night or even every other night, but maybe every week or two, she'd be going to another show. We got after her for keeping it such a secret. She always was that way, never saying much about herself, but we finally got her to break down and admit she had a boy friend. She wouldn't tell us his name, though, only that it was 'Johnny.'

"That kept on all through the summer and we asked her if it was anything serious, but all she'd do was say, 'Who knows?' She never would tell us anything. She always wanted us to talk, but she wouldn't. We tried to get her to bring him up sometime, so we could meet him, but she never would and she wouldn't tell us a whisper about him, what he did, or how she met him, or anything. She wouldn't even tell us what he looked like. She'd always laugh and change the subject.

"Then, it was two or three months ago, she didn't go out any more. You could tell something had happened, because her face got longer and longer. We suspected they'd broken up, but we didn't dare ask her about it.

"Then, in January, like a bolt out of the blue, she suddenly said she was going to move out. It was only about ten days before the end of the month. At first she wouldn't say why. All she'd admit was she was quitting her job and leaving town, but we couldn't let her alone on that, so she finally broke down and said she was getting married. Well, we were utterly astonished. We asked if it was Johnny and she said it was and we couldn't get over it. We told her we thought that had broken up and she said it had for a while, but then he'd come back and proposed and they were going to get married right away.

"We were eager to help her get ready for the wedding, but she wouldn't have it. She said it was going to be a quiet affair and she didn't know where. She said Johnny had been transferred out West somewhere and she was going out there to marry him. She couldn't even tell us where she was going to live, she said, because she didn't know, and she wouldn't even tell us what her married name would be. All she'd say was that as soon as they were settled, she'd write and tell us all about it."

The girl brushed a hand over her forehead. "On that Friday night, the last Friday in January, she packed all her things and Saturday morning Bob came over in his truck and took the trunk to the station for her and she shipped it out. She left here on Sunday. She took a taxi to the station with those suitcases and that's the last we ever saw or heard of her."

Fellows stroked his chin when the girl's story was finished. He had expected that when he learned the victim's identity, he'd automatically discover the man's, but it hadn't come so easily. The man, whoever he was, had operated completely under cover, had apparently sold Joan Simpson a fast line and convinced her he should never be revealed.

When Ruth's roommate, Helen Burnam, came in with Bob Herald, Fellows and Wilks questioned them with the same effect. Helen, no more than Ruth, knew anything about the dead girl's background, only that she worked for the Fizz-Rite Bottling Company, and she too knew nothing more than "Johnny's" first name. Bob Herald had little additional information. "I took her trunk to the station," he said. "She rode with me and I kept asking her where she was going, but she wouldn't say. She wouldn't even let me see when she filled out a tag for the trunk. She kept saying I'd find out all about it in good time. I thought it was a funny way for a girl about to get married to behave and I guess I was half thinking she wasn't going to get married at all. I sort of suspected she was running away with some guy."

When the two policemen left, Wilks went down the stairs a frustrated man. "What was the matter with that girl?" he growled. "Couldn't she see she was playing right into the hands of a murderer?"

Fellows said, "Are you figuring he meant to kill her from the first moment, Sid?"

Wilks banged the suitcase he carried against the rail of the concrete steps outside in anger. "What do you figure?"

Fellows shook his head. "I guess I figure the ceiling needs a few more BB's before it falls," he said, and Wilks gave him a puzzled look.

Wednesday morning Sergeant Wilks made a trip to the Fizz-Rite Bottling Company south of Townsend and talked to everyone there who could give him information about the late Joan Simpson. At the same time, Ed Lewis was put in charge of a new project, that of checking every motel in the prescribed area for guests by the name of John Campbell. That morning, too, Raymond Watly made another trip to Hartford and his was the dreariest job of all. Since Andy Palekowski had seen Burchard and not Campbell, all the rogue's gallery pictures he had checked had to be gone over again. Frank Restlin complained and Watly was unhappy, but it was work that had to be done.

Wilks was back from his job before lunch and reported to the chief that Fizz-Rite company records showed Joan Simpson had been in their employ since September 1954, that she had worked in the Bridgeport production plant until September 1957, when she was among those moved to the new bottling plant just opened outside of Townsend. Before that, Joan had worked for the Masters Toy Company in Bridgeport and her family had their home in that city. As for the question of men in her life, no one there admitted knowing a thing. No one there had ever tried to date her.

"That girl was too quiet for her own good," Wilks complained. "Somewhere in her life there's a man, but it's a better secret than the atom bomb."

Fellows said, "Sure nobody was lying, Sid?"

"I can't swear to it. Who can? But there are only twelve men in the plant and nine of them are married and the three single ones are in their early twenties and all three are going steady."

"And the married men?"

"I didn't see them all. There's her boss, of course, a guy named Donald Jones, and he knows her the best, but he's forty and doesn't fit the description of Campbell. I made a point of meeting all the men I could and finding out about the others. There are only two there who do fit it." He pulled his notebook from his pocket and flipped the pages. "One is Benjamin Hamper, married, three children, lives in Stamford. The other is Henry Callen, married, no children. He lives in Townsend. Hamper claims he never even knew Joan Simpson and Callen only knew her slightly. And neither of them ever worked for Gary Hardware in Erie."

"Erie?" Fellows reflected at the name. "I think maybe we should forget about Erie." He sifted briefly through the papers on his desk. "I got a report today, if I can find it." He gave up. "Anyway, the Erie police have checked everybody they can find out there who knows their John Campbell and they can't trace any connection at all."

"Meaning what? That it's another coincidence?"

"That's my guess. The guy picks Gary Hardware because he saw the name somewhere. He gets 'John Campbell' out of the air and it so happens there really is a John Campbell there. That's not such a rare name and the plant employs six thousand people."

"And that ex-employee, Richard Lester was cleared.

What about the other five names they gave you?"

"They've been cleared too. I got the last of that to-day too."

Wilks sat down and pulled out his tobacco. "What you're trying to say is you don't have anybody at all, is that it?"

"Right now it's just those two men at the plant you mentioned, Hamper and Callen." Fellows smiled. "It's not much, is it?"

"It's nothing," Wilks said, biting tobacco and offering it to the chief. "I even tried that business about anything special happening at the plant last spring, back last April or May. You know, somebody coming in for a while, someone she might have met? That's when she started dating. Her boss checked the records to see what purchasing agents showed up at that time. That's really reaching for straws, because how the hell is she going to get that acquainted with some guy dropping in once?"

"You got those names?"

"Yep. William Sedgewick. He made two calls because he sells to them regularly. There were two others. Robert Coffin and Kenneth Worley. Sedgewick you can rule out because he's blond and heavy. The other two called once, and the boss doesn't remember what they looked like. We can check on them through the companies they represent if you think it's worth while. I've got that dope."

"I don't think it's particularly worth while, but we'll do it."

"It's a waste of time, but all right." Wilks made notes and said, "So we check them and find they're clean and then we have nothing."

"Not quite nothing." Fellows stared up at his picture gallery. "You know," he said, turning, "Joan Simpson met that man somehow. Now if it wasn't through the office, how was it?"

"She runs into an old friend on the street."

"Maybe an old friend, or maybe a new one. Remember, Burchard never set eyes on her before, and in twenty minutes he's in bed with her."

"You mean she's a sucker for any guy?"

"I'd guess not quite any guy, Sid, but we do know she was something of a pushover, not eager, but not unwilling. If she meets the right kind of guy, something clicks and off they go to the hay. That's what I think."

"Sounds all right, but what does it get us?"

Fellows shrugged. "It gets us the possibility that maybe her 'Johnny' made his connection the same way Burchard did. He rang her doorbell to sell her something."

"When's she home?"

"On a weekend when it so happens the other girls are away, or at night, Sid!" His eyes lighted. "At night. The other girls are out and Joan is home. He rings the bell. He's selling something."

Wilks gave him a quizzical smile. "Trying to make a quota, Fred?"

"People sell at night, Sid. My boy is trying to pick up money right now selling storm windows. He does that after school and in the evening sometimes." He tilted his chair back and stared at space. "He works during the day. He's got a job. In the evenings he works doing door-to-door selling."

Wilks wasn't impressed. "That's one way he could meet her. There're a hundred others."

"But this way explains things that I don't think any of the others would. For instance, we guess he's married. We guess he then must work evenings because he had to have some kind of excuse to see Joan every night. Going out selling could be the job."

"It could be," Wilks admitted. "You're taking a lot for granted, but it could be."

"And he'll bear a fair resemblance to Clyde Burchard."

Wilks laughed. "Now your reasoning is getting over my head."

"The picture that girl drew for us wasn't a good resemblance, but both Watly and Andy said it looked slightly like the guy."

"But Andy never saw Campbell. It was Burchard he saw."

"Andy didn't, but Watly did. Figure it this way, Sid. Andy was trying to get the girl to draw a picture of Burchard, and Watly was trying to get her to draw Campbell. What they probably got was something in between. It probably looks as much like Campbell as it does Burchard."

Wilks stretched and disclaimed interest. "Personally I didn't think it looked much like Burchard. I wouldn't have picked him out of any line-up on the strength of it."

"I thought it did a little around the eyes."

"Not much."

"It's something to consider. Then, of course, there're the motels."

"What motels?"

Fellows told him what he was having Lewis do. "Look at it this way, Sid. From what we know, this guy is a chronic philanderer. A guy like that needs a place, doesn't he? Motels are great for it."

Wilks had to admit it. "Let's hope he uses the name Campbell," he said.

"And meanwhile, you and I can keep busy. Now that we know who Joan's parents are, I guess it's time to let them know about her. You can see what you can learn at the Fizz-Rite main company in Bridgeport, and I'll talk to her folks. I guess it's about time somebody told them what happened to their daughter."

Mr. and Mrs. Robert Simpson lived on Eastview Avenue in Bridgeport, a lower-class suburban street whose houses were old, but whose trees were older, consisting of full-grown maples and elms, their naked branches jigsawing the sky. The Simpson place was a two-story, one-family house in need of paint. There was a postage stamp lawn crusted with the remains of Monday's snow and an icy driveway to a tumbledown garage in the rear.

Fellows looked the house over and took a deep breath when he got out of the car. This was the second time in the case he had approached a house prepared to explain to anguished parents that their daughter was dead and he relished it even less this time.

A man in a T shirt and house slippers answered the door and allowed that he was Mr. Simpson. Fellows introduced himself and the man let him in, his stern face, under a shock of iron-gray hair, showing perplexity and a little disquiet. Mr. Simpson didn't think he had broken any laws, but he couldn't imagine why else a policeman should be at the door.

Mrs. Simpson entered the living room wiping her hands on an apron and was equally uneasy upon learning the identity of the caller. Where her husband was a big man, as tall as Fellows himself, rock-ribbed and solid, she was short and had once been petite, though now she was running to fat. The two of them perched on chairs, leaning forward and waiting for whatever axe was to fall, and the chief, dangling his hat between his legs in an opposite chair, stared down at the floor. "You have a daughter Joan?"

The father exhaled, and his tension relaxed a little. He hadn't broken any laws after all. His wife sat a little farther forward, as if the tension he lost had been added to hers. "Yes," she said in a quiet, strained voice.

"I want to talk to you about her," Fellows said, trying in his mind to phrase his sentences.

It was Mr. Simpson who spoke then. "She got herself into trouble, didn't she?"

"I'm afraid so."

"I'm not surprised," the man snapped. "She's a tramp."

"She's a good girl," his wife said defensively.

"It was with a man, wasn't it?" Simpson said.

"Yes."

"That's what I thought. She's a no-good tramp. That's what I told her and that's what I told you. Whatever she done she deserves what she gets."

Fellows changed his approach a little. "Why do you say that?"

"She don't live how we bring her up. Men! She's always playing around with a man."

His wife said, "Now, Robert, you don't know that."

"What do you mean I don't know it?" he said back. "I do know it. How about that guy in the toy company? You think she got those presents because she took shorthand good?"

"What man was that?" the chief asked.

Mrs. Simpson said, with hot tears in her eyes, "That's no way to talk about your daughter. Especially to strangers. Joan was a good girl." She turned to Fellows. "She was always good to us. She was nice to have around. Never an unkind word, never any fights—"

"We had fights," Simpson said. "Her and I."

"It was you who did it. Hitting at her because she wanted a good time. What's being young for, but to have a good time?"

"She didn't have to go shacking up with her boss. That's not the way a girl should behave. I told her and told her she'd have to pay the price."

"She was a good girl. The only thing wrong was you not talking to her, except when you had wine and you wanted to fight."

"She didn't deserve I should talk with her. Would she go to church? Would she act decent like I wanted her to? No."

Mrs. Simpson turned her attention to the chief. "What kind of trouble is she in?"

Fellows would have stalled, but the question was direct and there was no way to avoid an answer. "We think she's been killed," he said quietly.

Both parents said, "No!" together, and Mrs. Simpson leaned still farther forward. "That can't be."

"We found a body," the chief said, "which has been tentatively identified as being a Joan Simpson, who worked for the Fizz-Rite Company in Townsend. We've been told you are her parents."

Mr. Simpson's heavily lined face crinkled up. A choking sob came out of his mouth and tears started from the creases that hid his eyes. "My baby," he cried. "My Joan." He began to sob and stumbled blindly out of the room, his cries echoing back through the house until a door slammed.

Mrs. Simpson sat perfectly still for a long time, staring vacantly into space, her only movements being a gentle rocking and the twisting of her fingers in her lap. Then she looked painfully at Fellows. "Is there—any chance of a mistake?"

Fellows said, "Of course, until your husband or you view the remains it's not positive, but I'm afraid there isn't much question."

She nodded and stared emptily once more. "You—said—someone killed her?"

"We believe so."

"Did—you—catch him?"

"No, ma'am. We're trying to. I'm hoping you can help us."

"Of course we'll help." She was silent a moment and then said, "Please excuse my husband. He really loved her very much."

"I never doubted that." Fellows made a move to get up. "If you'd rather I came back later—"

"No," she said. "It's—I don't mind talking about her. I'd like to talk about her."

"Maybe you could tell me something about her life, particularly from high school on."

Mrs. Simpson nodded and started. She talked at length, and to a large extent irrelevantly, as if recollecting her only child's life for her own sustenance, purging herself of the temptations of grief by remembering. Fellows made no effort to stop her, to direct her along the lines that interested him. He let her ramble for her own good and for the possible chance that something, apparently unconnected, might be a clue to what happened to her later.

Joan Simpson had always lived in their present house. In childhood she went to the neighborhood school and on to Bassick High, where she graduated in 1946. There followed two years in the Junior College of Commerce in New Haven, learning shorthand and typing, where she proved herself a more than capable student. Mrs. Simpson demonstrated her point by getting Joan's high school and Junior College diplomas, and Fellows was properly impressed. After that, Joan got a job in an accounting firm, but didn't care much for it and in October of 1950 took another job as private secretary to E. M. Busso, Vice President of the Masters Toy Company. "My husband thinks she wasn't a nice girl with Mr. Busso," she said. "I don't think that's right. We met Mr. Busso many times when he came to take Joan out and he was always a gentleman. He was very rich, but he didn't talk down to us at all. He was nice to us and he thought the world of Joan. Just because he gave her some presents—he could afford them. He gave us that television set one Christmas. He was a very nice man. I always hoped," she said sadly, "that perhaps he and Joan would get married, even if he was a lot older. That didn't happen and I guess it's because he looked on Joan more like a daughter. He was very nice to young girls trying to get ahead. When he let Joan go, which was in June back, let me see, I believe it was 1954, when he let her go, it was to give a new young girl a chance. As he explained it to Joan, she was ready for better things. Joan was quite bitter, but I'm sure Mr. Busso knew best."

Fellows said, "Your husband didn't share your view that Mr. Busso was—a father to Joan?"

"I think my husband was jealous because Mr. Busso did such nice things for her. My husband wouldn't hardly talk to Joan. All the time she worked for Mr. Busso, which was nearly four years, she lived with us and he wouldn't say hardly anything except to call her a tramp or sometimes worse things. But Joan was a good girl. She lived with us. She didn't have her own apartment."

After her release from Masters Toys, Joan spent several months idling around, doing nothing. She went on a Nassau cruise that summer on her savings and stayed around the house the rest of the time until after Labor Day. "She didn't think Mr. Busso treated her fairly," Mrs. Simpson said. "She didn't know it was for her own good, because Mr. Busso was a nice man and wealthy and gave us presents and a man like that wouldn't do anything that wasn't right."

That fall she hunted for a job again and obtained one with the Fizz-Rite Company in town and continued to live at home and at odds with her father until she was transferred to the newly-opened branch bottling plant. She bought a secondhand car and commuted the first few weeks, then sold the car and moved to Townsend, taking a furnished room in a boarding house, the name of which Mrs. Simpson couldn't remember. It was a temporary arrangement, for she wasn't happy with it and when she had the opportunity to move in with two other girls in a two-bedroom apartment, she took it.

"We didn't see her often after she sold her car," Mrs. Simpson said. "Where she lived wasn't so far away, but it takes a long time by train. She had to catch the local into Stamford or take a bus and then get the train to Bridgeport. I guess it was hard for her, especially with her father so dead set against her. I thought maybe she might buy another car, but she wouldn't because she wasn't making as much money and her new boss wasn't generous, like Mr. Busso, and didn't give her presents."

The one thing Fellows noted that Mrs. Simpson had overlooked in her long and detailed recital, were men in Joan's life. He asked about that. "Oh, she had dates," Mrs. Simpson said. "When she was in school, she was very popular. The boys used to line up for her then. Of course, when she went to business college she didn't have as much time for dates, but she had quite a few. After she got her job, though, it was different. I guess she didn't meet so many single men. There were a few, of course. When she first went to work for Masters some of the men there took her out, but then they stopped for some reason or other. One by one they dropped out." She said sadly, "I think perhaps Joan was hoping too much to marry Mr. Busso. I think maybe she discouraged those other boys from coming around. I think maybe she shouldn't have. She should have known Mr. Busso was only interested in seeing her get ahead."

Wilks and Fellows compared notes over coffee in a Bridgeport diner in the middle of the afternoon. Fellows related the details of his interview with Mrs. Simpson and said, "The husband came back in before I left. They're going to view the body and take care of the funeral business. And I stopped in at headquarters. Not a whisper on the Jean Sherman angle. No calls. He hasn't been near the house. Not a sign."

Wilks said, "You want my opinion? The guy is a ghost. He doesn't really exist at all."

"It's a ghost we'd better find or maybe we won't exist. You pick up anything at Fizz-Rite?"

"I learned that three guys there had dated her at one time or another. I talked to one of them. The other two were out on the road. They're salesmen."

"They got dark hair?"

"One has. Guy named Manners. I didn't see him, but there isn't going to be anything there. He and his family own a house in here, so he could hardly be making the trip to Stockford at the times we hear Campbell was there."

"Don't bet on it."

"All right," Wilks said in distaste. "We'll put him on the list of suspects. That makes the list about one."

"What about the other two?"

"The other salesman is a blond and the one I talked to is in between. His name is DeKeyser. He said he took Joan out about three times but then laid off because she had her hooks out. He said two dates and she started acting like she owned him. Three, and he could see the altar staring him in the face and that was enough. Same with the others, or so he told me. Manners started dating her shortly after she started working there, but after a few weeks he quit. Then DeKeyser took her out and had the same experience. He and Manners got talking about it after and that's why he knew that story. Then it was the blond guy and he had the same trouble. He stopped seeing her, but it didn't end there for either of them. She kept making plays for them long after they had crossed her off the list with the result that it got embarrassing. He didn't come out and say so, but he led me to believe one of the reasons she was transferred to the new plant was to get her out of their hair."

Fellows was silent for a few seconds before saying, "Maybe Campbell wasn't as lucky as the others. I presume those men weren't married."

"Not when they were dating her. DeKeyser is now."

"I guess she got in Campbell's hair too, wanting to get married. I guess he must have rented that house to placate her and keep her quiet."

"Meaning he had a wife she was threatening to go see?"

"Sounds like it. Maybe she thought she could persuade him to divorce her. You notice she wouldn't tell her roommates what her married name would be. If she was merely going to live with him for a while and call it quits, she wouldn't have to act like that. She'd give them some name and never see them again. Her promising to write them all about it sounds as if she really expected to get married, as if she could come back and parade a wedding ring. She didn't want them to know her as Mrs. Campbell, not if she could hitch onto his real name."

Wilks shook his head. "Now that's good theorizing, Fred, or at least I guess it is, but what's the use of it? That doesn't move us one inch closer to this guy."

"Sometimes theories help, Sid. By theorizing, you can sometimes guess what a man's going to do next and intercept him at it. You get a picture of the man and his habits even if you can't put your finger on him."

"You can have all the pictures you want. All I'm after is the real McCoy."

Fellows reached in his pocket and put out a tip. "Well, let's go talk to some of the guys at Masters Toy Company while we're here and see what we can learn."

"You aren't going to find the real McCoy in some place she worked at eight years ago, are you?"

"I don't expect so, but we're going to look anyway. That's what the detective business is all about."

Mr. Busso of the Masters Toy Company was a stout man whose hair was almost gone, but advancing age, receding hair, and encroaching fat didn't remove the air of the lecher he wore as a permanent badge of his bachelorhood. His secretary, a pretty young thing who had acquired an expensive wardrobe after only six months of work, showed the two policemen into his luxurious office and he welcomed them with a patronizing air. "It's a shame about Joan," he said with reference to their phone call. "Of course I'll help any way I can, but I don't know what I could tell you. I haven't seen her since she left here."

Mr. Busso was agreeable in manner, but his general statements as to his acquaintance with the deceased weren't of assistance. She had been a capable secretary and a fine young woman. He had no complaints about her work and gave her a high recommendation when she left. On the subject that mattered, the men in her life, he denied any knowledge. "I don't think she had many dates," he said. "I certainly doubt whoever did her in ever worked for us."

"She never dated anyone here?" Fellows asked.

"I'm sure she didn't."

"This is certain knowledge on your part?"

Busso backed off. "Now, of course, I can't be certain. I didn't run her social life."

"We've had it from other sources that some of the people here did date her when she started work."

Busso worked his lips thoughtfully. "Well now, I guess that's right. I guess she did have a few dates. I guess a couple of the men here took her out."

"Which men?"

"Well, I wouldn't know."

"You mean it was a secret? The men didn't want you to know?"

"Of course not. I don't mean that at all."

"Then if it wasn't a secret and you knew she went out, you must have known who took her out."

Busso hemmed and hawed a moment or two. "I know one," he finally said. "Fellow by the name of Lawrence. Used to be in sales. He chased her quite a bit. He wasn't with us long though."

"Lawrence? Know where he lives?"

"I only know his name is John Lawrence. Personnel might still have him listed. He was a Bridgeport man."

"John, huh? Can you tell us what he was like? Describe him?"

"He was a young fellow, late twenties. About six feet tall, slender build, dark hair. I suppose you'd call him nice-looking."

"Any others?"

Busso's manner had lost a little of its geniality. His

brows were darker and his eyes were thoughtful. He said abruptly, "I don't know of any others."

"This might help," Fellows said, rising. "Where would I find personnel?"

"Third door on your right, down the hall." Busso got up too. "I'd look into Lawrence. He might have carried on with her after he left here. He's the type."

Wilks grinned at Fellows as they got into the hall. "Somebody was beating his time, I guess."

Fellows said, "There wasn't any love lost there, that's for sure."

The personnel manager, a Mr. Blake, was available, and they sat down with him in his office to tell him their story. He listened and looked sympathetic at news of Joan's death, but grinned at the mention of Lawrence.

"I remember the whole thing," he said. "I ought to. Joan was one of Busso's girls. He buys a new edition about every four years. They're always bright, shiny, and eye-catching, but everyone around here knows you don't touch the merchandise. This fellow Lawrence, though, he was working here when Busso brought in Joan Simpson. Lawrence was in sales, that's right across the hall, so I knew him quite well. He was a character, that boy. No woman between six and sixty was safe around him.

"He hadn't been in here long, though, and Joan was brought in a short time after to replace one of Busso's older models. Old John knew he shouldn't touch, of course, he was savvy enough to know the score, but she was right up his alley, real Lawrence bait, and then there was the challenge. That was partly it too, I guess. Anyway, he went after Joan himself, hot and heavy and, of course, alongside of Busso, this guy was prince charming. Joan knew the score too and she was playing both ends against the middle, holding hands with

Busso, so to speak, on top of the table and playing footsie with Lawrence underneath.

"But that Busso, say what you like, he was still no dummy and this kind of thing couldn't go on long without him catching wise. When he did, out went Lawrence. The rest of us around here thought he'd can them both, but as I say, Busso isn't a real dummy. Joan he liked, Lawrence he didn't, so it was Lawrence who got the gate and that broke up the affair nice and clean. After that, Busso had no more trouble."

Fellows said, "This lad Lawrence sounds like a guy who can't stay away from the women no matter what the risk."

Mr. Blake, who wasn't too old a man himself, laughed. "I'd say he not only wouldn't stay away no matter what the risk, he'd go looking no matter what the risk. You think he had anything to do with it?"

"The attitude fits. Know what happened to him? Know if he kept on seeing Joan?"

"I don't think he did. He might have tried, but I think Busso would make it clear to Joan what her position was and she'd play safe. I don't know about that. I did run into him on the street a couple of years later and we didn't talk about Joan. He was the kind of guy who could forget a girl pretty fast. My guess is that trying to keep on with her when he wasn't working there would be complicated. I think he'd look around where he was, rather than waste effort on hard-to-get girls."

"You don't know where he is now?"

"That time I saw him on the street he said he was selling cars. Of course that was six years ago or longer. I don't know where he'd be now."

"Anything in your files on him?"

Blake had his secretary check through the records. She came back with nothing. "You'd probably find him in the phone book," the personnel manager said.

Fellows said, "If we do, he's probably not the man."
He and Wilks thanked him and went out.

John Lawrence was not in the Bridgeport phone book nor was he listed in Townsend, Stockford, or any of the other neighboring towns that Fellows had included in his "area." This fact awakened the chief's interest, but didn't have the same effect on the detective sergeant. "He could be anywhere," Wilks said. "He lost his job and sold cars for a while and then got another job up in Maine or out in Podunk, Iowa. Just because—"

"I know all that," Fellows told him. "I just want to find out."

It was Thursday morning and the reports on the chief's desk were mostly negative. A check of pawn shops had failed to produce the wrist watch Burchard claimed Joan was wearing; a check of motel registers had failed to turn up the name John Campbell; and Watly's second trip to Hartford had been as fruitless as the first. In addition, there were reports from the State Police lab saying that while fingerprints had been found on some of the silver taken from the murder house, they were unidentified and presumably belonged to the dead girl. Dust from the house had been analyzed and found clueless. The only positive development in the case was a report from Dr. MacFarlane saying that Mr. and Mrs. Simpson had identified the body as being their daughter and had taken it home for burial.

Wilks gestured at the cluttered desk and said, "You're getting desperate, Fred. You're desperate so you're going after an eight-year-old affair that has nothing to show it's held over at all."

"I'm going after everything everywhere," Fellows admitted, "but it's not because I'm desperate. I'm trying to be thorough."

Fellows's thoroughness in this matter consisted of sending a team of three men to Bridgeport to make inquiries of all automobile franchises and another team to cover the motels again, this time to a hunt for John Lawrences. And when Hilders of the Bridgeport *Courier* came in, Fellows, after telling him a lot of nothings, said suddenly, "How long have you lived in Bridgeport, Mr. Hilders?"

"Me? All my life."

"Ever know or hear of a man named John Lawrence?"

It was a shot in the dark, like most of Fellows's shots these days and like most of the others, it didn't hit anything. Hilders blinked and said, "No. Why?"

"Skip it. It doesn't matter."

"Skip it?" Hilders laughed. "Are you kidding? You think Lawrence is Campbell's real name, don't you?"

"Off the record, we think it might be, but remember, Mr. Hilders. That is off the record. I don't want that name mentioned in any of your articles."

Hilders grumbled that his paper wanted news of the case, that he was supposed to collect stories, but anything that happened was kept a dark secret. Fellows reminded him that he had scooped the other papers on the identity of the victim. "Don't forget, Hilders, I called you last night before I called the wire services. I gave you a break, so you play ball."

"You called me, but too late for the last edition. It came out this morning and it was in all the other papers too."

"Well, if you're after exclusives, why don't you check on funeral arrangements instead of hanging around here?"

He got rid of Hilders that way, but the reporter's visit didn't help the chief's mood. He spent the rest of the morning poring over the reports and drinking coffee, sitting sullenly silent at his desk trying to find new avenues to test, new leads to follow.

At eleven, Harris called from Bridgeport. A careful check of all auto dealers, used and new, past and present, had failed to reveal anyone named John Lawrence in that field over the last ten years. It looked as if once again the chief had drawn a blank.

Half an hour later, however, he got a piece of news that reversed his views. Wilson, one of the men assigned to the motel detail called in. "John Lawrence, Chief. This time you got it! A John Lawrence checked in at the Cozy Cove motel south of Townsend on December nineteenth. 'Mr. and Mrs. John Lawrence,' the card says."

The chief smiled for the first time that day. "Any home address?"

"Yes, a phoney. I checked it."

Fellows liked that. His smile broke into a grin. "Bring in that card. I want his handwriting."

By the time Wilson returned with the motel registration card, three other reports had come in. A John Lawrence was found to have registered on December second at the Bide-a-Bit motel south of Danbury, at the Cozy Rest, east of Townsend on November eighteenth, and at the Post motel on route one east of Stamford on January fifteenth. The same false address was listed each time.

When Wilks returned at three-thirty that afternoon,

Fellows was walking on wires. "Campbell is Lawrence," the chief said, relating the day's events. "I know it as sure as I'm born." He clapped Wilks on the shoulder. "And you couldn't see why we should investigate the toy company."

Wilks was less inclined to enthusiasm, especially since he was shown up as wrong. "So what's that prove?"

"What do you mean what's it prove? It proves plenty."

Wilks sat down in the chief's chair and tilted it back. "The trouble with you, Fred, is you haven't been eating enough and it's making you dizzy. John Lawrence is just as phoney as his addresses. We don't know who John Lawrence is any more than we know who John Campbell is, so what's finding out another alias do for us?"

Fellows hooked a leg over the corner of his table and grinned. "I'll tell you what it does. It tells us Joan Simpson used to know the man she rented the house with. Busso broke it up and they didn't see each other after that for nearly eight years and then they met again—"

"Now wait a minute!"

"Sure. Joan didn't have any dates and no boy friends and suddenly she takes up with a guy. Obviously they hadn't been seeing each other and somehow happened to meet. Now, where's a calendar?" Fellows made a half-hearted effort to find one in his pile of papers, gave up, and said, "Never mind. But I checked those motel dates. One is a Friday, two are Tuesdays, and one's a Thursday. This Campbell or Lawrence or whatever his real name is is free any night in the week. Therefore, if he's married, it's certain he has some evening job."

"Or he isn't married," said Wilks, "and doesn't work nights at all. You're making unwarranted assumptions just because he used a phoney name."

"But if he isn't married," said Fellows, grinning, "why wouldn't he have his girls come to his apartment? He wouldn't have to rent motel rooms."

Wilks laughed and shook his head. "God, Sherlock Holmes again, reading a man's life history from the dents in his watch. You could be all wet, you know."

"I'll be wrong on some things, but, by God, I'll be right on most. You wait and see."

"All right. What else are you going to be right on?"

"I think he's got a jail record."

"Oh, he has? What about Watly being all through the mug files and not finding him?"

"There are forty-seven other states he could have a record in. Forty-eight now, including Alaska."

"All right, Mr. Bones. Tell me why you think he's got a record."

"Because he uses the name Lawrence not only signing in at motels, but he also used it when he worked for the toy company. A man would only use an alias if he were hiding a record." Fellows waved a hand. "And don't say it's his real name, because you're the one who said it wasn't."

"Maybe I'm wrong. It's been known to happen."

"But if it was his real name, Sid, then we'd have turned him up as working as a car salesman in Bridgeport six years ago. If he was a car salesman, then he sold them under another name."

"Or he lied to Blake about selling cars."

"Why?"

Wilks shrugged. "There could be plenty of reasons we don't know about. All right, anything else?"

"Well, it's obvious he's a salesman. Everything points to that. The evidence also suggests he does some selling at night. Night selling would probably be door to door on his own, since he can take nights off and wouldn't have to account to a wife for not making money. So it's, as I've said before, quite probable he met Joan on a house call one evening when her roommates were out, the only difference being that he'd known her before."

"All right. That's possible, even probable."

"And Townsend is one of his territories, but he doesn't live there."

"He doesn't live in Townsend?" Wilks blinked. "I can't wait to hear this explanation."

"It's easy. He wouldn't rent a motel room where he might be known, would he? Here." He pulled out an area road map from his papers. "I drew five mile circles around each motel he stopped at. This is reaching, I'll admit, but if he wouldn't stop at a motel within five miles of his home, Townsend is excluded."

Wilks studied the four circles. Danbury was enclosed and the whole Stamford-Townsend area. The rest was open and available. The detective sergeant shrugged. "Even if you're right, Fred, you don't eliminate much."

"But when all the reports are in, then I'll circle the motels where he isn't listed and maybe we can kind of pinpoint his location. If we should find he's hit all the motels in a certain section but one, the chances are he'll live near that one."

Wilks shook his head, somewhat in awe. "Brother. What rabbits you pull out of what hats." He sat back. "You know, Fred, I'll bet you're so wrapped up in these surmises you haven't even thought of the logical way of finding the guy."

"Which is what?"

"Getting these motel owners to report in the next time a John Lawrence signs a card."

"We're doing that, Sid. The last time was January fifteenth, but after that he was mixed up with this Joan Simpson and nothing's happened since. But he'll start in again. We'll watch and we may get him, but we aren't passing up our other chances."

"Which are what?"

"We check with Washington for a crook with a John

Lawrence alias and we're going to have all the police departments around investigate all men with a reputation as a libertine. As you say, Sid, I may be all wet on a lot of these suppositions, but I'm not going to be wrong on all of them and one of the right ones is going to turn up our boy."

Chief Fred Fellows was, at the least, inventive, but the
bad luck that seemed to dog him on the case held up
against his best efforts. None of the answers he felt he
had to get were forthcoming. The Federal Bureau of
Investigation reported no known criminals who used
the aliases John Lawrence or John Campbell, or at
least none who could possibly be involved in the Simpson case. Photostats of the handwriting, or rather the
printing John Lawrence had scrawled onto motel cards
had arrived, but trying to match it was reported as an
impossible task. In short, Washington could give nothing but negative information.

Negative information was all that resulted from the
search for known libertines. Two possibilities had been
shown to Watly who ruled them out without hesitation.

The bitterest blow was struck Friday night. The editor of the Bridgeport *Courier* pulled reporter John Hilders off a case that produced so little interest, and
Hilders, no longer needing the good graces of Fred Fellows, blew the lid off in his article. BRIDGEPORT
GIRL MADE LOVE IN MURDER HOUSE was the
headline and the story, which all readers were sure to
devour, revealed all that Hilders knew and suspected.

The girl's name wasn't disclosed only because the reporter couldn't find it out, but the fact the police knew who she was and were watching her house was boldly shouted to the public. The worst blow of all, however, was the revelation that the police had information the mysterious John Campbell was known by another name and that name was John Lawrence.

It was an article that brought thirty curiosity calls to Bridgeport police headquarters and a dozen more from reporters who assailed both them and the Stockford police with questions. The police refused to comment on the story, but Fellows knew denials were useless and the *Courier* information was repeated in all other papers the following morning. It was a revelation that Mr. John Campbell-Lawrence could hardly miss and it insured the futility of catching the man in the traps the police had set.

Fellows didn't go into a towering rage at the publication of the information. He banned Hilders and any other representatives of the *Courier* from police headquarters forever, but other than that, he shook his head dispiritedly, either at the deceit of his fellow man or at the elimination of what looked like the best hope for catching John Campbell.

As the other negative news came in on Saturday he grew quieter, drank more coffee, and shuffled the papers on his office desk a little aimlessly. Motel reports had produced no registrations in addition to the original four, so he couldn't even pursue his pinpoint plan any further and for that day there was nothing more to do.

In the middle of the afternoon Wilks tried to cheer him up, but it was a fruitless process. "It's the breaks of the game, Fred," he said. "Not every case gets solved."

Fellows said, "What's that supposed to do, make everything all right?"

"You've done everything you could, and more than most. All that stratosphere stuff! That's more than I'd have thought of."

"All of that stratosphere stuff looks kind of cockeyed now, doesn't it? But I guess it did to you all along."

"You just put too much store in it. That's why you feel let down."

Fellows swung his chair around. "That's not why I feel let down. What gets me down is that murder is the worst crime there is and this is murder and we know it and I don't like to see a murderer, of all criminals, get away with his crime."

"Seventy percent of them do, Fred."

"You still don't make me feel better. Sure seventy percent of the murders go unsolved, and that's why there's so much murder. Every time the police have to throw in the sponge on a killing, it means the temptation for another man to kill is just a little stronger. Every time a slayer gets caught and punished, it makes the temptation for others just a little less. Someone's life might be saved by our catching this man."

Wilks sat down and put a hand on Fellows's shoulder. "Listen, Fred, you're getting worked up and you can't. You're all the time cutting out too wide. You think about meanings and stuff like that the same way you think of clues, not for what they represent, but in some fourth dimension."

Fellows managed a wry smile. "What are you talking about?"

"You and your reaching. We find the name Campbell is a phoney and you aren't content with the obvious reason, which is that he wants to hide his identity. You try to read into it that his wife nags him, or that he's got five kids or something. Now you take this thing. You've done everything you can and it doesn't work out. You ought to shake it off. It's not your fault, so stop worrying about what effect failure is going to have on society. What happens here isn't going to stop or start any new murders."

"It does, though," Fellows growled. "If every murder were solved and every murderer punished, premeditated murder would be wiped out."

"And you want to work towards such a day. You can't, so forget it. You've done your best. Nobody blames you. Nobody else could have done more. Stop thinking you ought to be Superman."

Fellows shook his head. "I'm not satisfied. I don't think it *is* my best. I think that somewhere, if I'd thought differently, or felt differently, we might have got onto a right track." He looked up. "There's no such thing as a perfect murder, Sid. There's always a track that leads from the killed back to the killer and no matter how well that killer covers that track, he's going to leave new tracks—tracks to the cover. And if he covers those, there'll be tracks to that cover and so on. There's always a flaw and the so-called 'perfect crime' means nothing more than that the police failed to find the flaw." He gestured at the mass of papers on his desk, the reports and information on the case. "There's a flaw in that mess somewhere. I don't know what or where, but there's got to be." He started to pick them up one by one, putting them together. "You know what I think I'll do, Sid? I'm going to take these home and study them. Maybe I can think of something."

Saturday evening Fred Fellows dropped in on his detective sergeant. Wilks was in his cellar working on model trains when the chief clumped down the stairs and ducked under the hanging light bulb at the bottom. "Marge said I'd find you here."

"I'm putting a caboose together." Wilks held it up. "How's that for realism?"

"Looks good. It also looks expensive."

"At least my wife knows where I am evenings." Wilks laid the car tenderly on his work table. "How're you feeling?"

"Hungry," Fellows said. "I don't mind cutting down on lunch and stuff, but my wife's getting into the act on dinners. She's taking it seriously."

"She's trying to help."

"That's the whole trouble. All the kids got a mountain of mashed potatoes and I got one tablespoonful. And I weigh more than any two of them together, except Larry."

"Come on, Fred. You didn't come over here to bum a sandwich. You've found a flaw."

"No flaws that I can spot, Sid. But I've got some ideas."

Wilks hitched his hip onto the table and pulled out his tobacco. "Shoot."

"This guy is a skirt chaser. Agreed?"

Wilks took a bite and passed the tobacco over. "That's obvious."

"Just. because one of his girl friends is dead, he's not going to reform."

Wilks nodded and accepted the packet back. "Equally obvious."

"And he lives somewhere in the area bounded by Stamford, Danbury, and Bridgeport."

Wilks shrugged. "That's not so obvious, but you're probably right. So do half a million other people."

"I see it like this, Sid. He works a regular job which gets him through at five o'clock. He picks up groceries and gets to the girl's house at five-thirty every night."

"Regular job? I thought you had him on the road selling."

"That's at night. His timing every day was too consistent for a road man. He'd be in an office of some kind, seems to me."

"I'll agree for kicks. Go on."

"If that's so, then he must work within a ten-minute drive of the murder house. That would mean Stockford, around the center of town. He couldn't be employed at the Grafton Tool and Die Company because it's too far away."

"Granting the assumption, the reasoning is valid. What does that prove?"

"If he worked in town before the murder, he still works here, or he's recently left a job here. This is going to be a rough assignment, Sid, but we're going to catalogue every single office and working man in the Stockford Center area. He's a white-collar man, judging from the reports. We believe he's a salesman, but he could be anything, a lawyer, a store clerk, pharmacist, possibly even a theater usher. It doesn't matter what he is, we're going to cover them all. We're going to get a list of employees from everybody who hires people in that area and we're going to check on them all. Any who might possibly fit the description we've got, we're going to have Watly look at. Any who've left town recently, we're going to track down. This is going to be a big job, but starting Monday every available man is going to be put to work on it. You and Ed Lewis will be in charge. That man is around here and we're going to find him."

"Well, let's say you're never at a loss for some new path to follow."

"Something has to break somewhere and it's got to be this."

"You mean you hope it'll be this."

"It's got to be, because if this fails, all that's left are two real brain teasers."

"Yeah?" Wilks was curious if not really interested. "What?"

"Why did he break into Restlin's office and steal the lease? That's one. The other is, why did he start to destroy the body and then stop and run?"

Wilks shrugged. "The answer to the first is that he didn't want us to have a copy of his signature. The answer to the second is he was afraid of discovery. Did you say brain teasers?"

"Brain teasers, Sid, because the answers to those answers are 'why?' and 'why?'. Why didn't he want us to have a copy of his handwriting? And what made him so scared he was going to be discovered?" Fellows smiled. "When you're not working tracking down people around town, you think about that. See if you can come up with anything."

"I can come up with something right now. He doesn't want us to have a sample of his handwriting, because he's somebody we're likely to investigate and this would damn him."

Fellows nodded. "That's just what I mean when I say he must work in this neighborhood. But, since Watly has seen him, he can be identified anyway, without the handwriting."

"Watly only saw him once, Fred. That identification might not stand up in court. The handwriting would. Or, if you think that makes the guy too bright and foresighted, he might not have intended killing the girl when he rented the house and it was only afterwards that he thought about covering up. Watly, he couldn't do anything about. The lease he could."

"And what about running off and leaving the body?"

Wilks munched on his tobacco carefully. He scratched the back of his neck. "Let's see. He starts burning the body in the furnace. Then, for some reason the furnace goes out and he can't start it again, so he switches to the fireplace. That creates such a stench he's afraid the neighbors will notice, so he quits."

"That's what we're apt to think, Sid, but it can't be the answer. A man bold enough to bring another woman to that house isn't going to run away and leave the job because the neighbors *might* notice. He'd have to have reason to believe the neighbors *did* notice. Remember, it's winter and all windows would be shut in everybody's houses."

"Maybe he couldn't stand the smell himself."

"Then he'd try something else, wouldn't he? He wouldn't just close up shop and skip. It seems to me he must have had some reason to believe he was about to be discovered."

"Some neighborhood kid poking around might have found something."

"Maybe. Seems like that's something we ought to try to find out."

Sunday through Wednesday 25

On Sunday Fellows worked long and hard with Wilks organizing the search that would be made of all downtown establishments. They got in Dudley Warner, the First Selectman, they got the Town Planning Commissioner and the head of the Chamber of Commerce. They plotted out the area from town maps, located and itemized the offices, stores, banks, theaters. They got the personnel managers of the two department stores in Stockford to bring in their lists of employees and made note of the departure of two men from their employ in the period they were interested in, the twentieth of February to the present time, and two policemen were sent to check the whereabouts of the missing two.

By the time the day was through, Fellows and Wilks had the operation pretty well worked out and the first thing Monday morning Raymond Watly was sent for and brought in. "This is the story," Fellows told him. "I have twenty-five policemen, every available patrolman and supernumerary, out on a door-to-door check of this whole area. We're convinced the man we're after works around here. You can stay in your office and conduct your business, but we want you available at any moment to go someplace and make an identification. Our men have the description you gave us. Every employee, manager, or worker is going to be looked at and any one who even vaguely resembles the man you saw is going to be shown to you. When an officer spots such a man, he will call in immediately. I have a driver standing by who will pick you up and take you there. The officer will point out the man in question and then it's up to you."

Watly was nervous at that. "It's been a long time, Chief. I only saw him that once. I don't want to have to say whether somebody I look at now might be the man I talked to six weeks ago. I don't want to be responsible. I don't remember him that well."

"This isn't a question of wanting, Mr. Watly. This man killed a woman. You remembered very well what he looked like when the case first broke and you remembered him well when the kid drew the picture, well enough to criticize the likeness. Now you aren't going to tell me you've suddenly forgotten what he looks like because I know that's not so. This is a duty and it's a duty only you can perform because you're the only one who's seen the man. I'm after a killer, Watly, and I'm not going to be thwarted because you're squeamish about putting the finger on him."

Watly chewed a lip. "That's what I'm worried about, Chief. I'm the only witness. I've got a wife and two little girls. If I'm the only man who can convict him for killing a woman, what's to stop him from killing me?"

"He's not going to touch you, Watly. You're going to be in the company of policemen at all times. The policemen will indicate the man in question and all you have to do is nod or shake your head. Now, there's nothing hard about that, is there?"

Watly said no, but he didn't sound convinced.

"One other thing. I want you to sit with me out on Center Street near the entrance of the cafeteria there during the noon hour. We're going to watch everyone

who goes in and out on the off chance our man might
be one of them."

"Yes, sir," Watly said without enthusiasm.

The first call came in then. It was Supernumerary
Pebble at Frank's Tobacco Store. "The employee here
could be it," he said. "In his thirties, dark, slender, tall.
I want Watly to see him."

Fellows hung up. "Your first victim," he told the
man. "Lambert," he called out to the driver in the
front room. "Here's Watly. It's Pebble at Frank's Tobacco. Center and South, northeast corner."

He shooed Watly into the waiting arms of the patrolman and went to study the map of the town spread out
on the table in his office. He marked the spot and made
notes.

The man in Frank's Tobacco Shop wasn't the one,
and Watly was returned to his office. Twice more he
was picked up and driven the short distance to some
new location for a look at another man and twice more
he shook his head.

At ten minutes of twelve it was Fellows who picked
him up. They drove over to the cafeteria and parked
in front of a hydrant a few yards short of the entrance.
"Don't take your eyes off that door," Fellows told him.
"We'll sit here till one o'clock when business slacks off
and then I'll take you in there to lunch."

Watly nodded and watched and said nothing.

"How about that man?" Fellows asked, gesturing.

"No."

"Not close?"

"No."

"That one?"

Watly shook his head. "What if he doesn't eat here?"

"Tomorrow we watch Manny's. Wednesday we watch
the Green Oak. Thursday we'll sit outside Harper's."

"How long will it take?"

"To canvass this whole area? Most of the week."

"What if you don't find him?"

"We'll find him. If he's here he won't get away. And he won't touch you, so stop being nervous."

They waited until after one without success and then they entered the cafeteria and ate lunch themselves, or at least Fellows ate. Watly had little appetite and toyed with a sandwich at the table the chief selected near the door. They watched each new customer, but by the time they left, when only a scattering of other diners still remained, the man they wanted had not come in.

Watly was called out four more times that afternoon, but the results were the same. The men he looked at were not John Campbell.

On Tuesday the systematic searching continued, and now the papers were picking up the case again. Rumors had spread that a hunt was on and the extraordinary procedures Chief Fellows had invoked were newsworthy. Six reporters showed up at headquarters that morning. Fellows, not an old hand at dealing with the press, nevertheless parried their questions well. Yes, they were canvassing the downtown area. No, he wouldn't reveal why he thought the mysterious John Campbell was located there. Yes, Raymond Watly was assisting in the investigation. No, he wouldn't predict what the results would be. There was a possibility, that was all.

Tuesday afternoon brought John Hilders back from Bridgeport, sneaking in and trying to mingle unobtrusively with the other reporters. He didn't come close to getting away with it. The chief pointed at the man and said, "You! Out!"

Hilders tried to protest, and Fellows broke him off. "My men have orders to chase you out of this town. Starting now, you have thirty seconds to take off."

Hilders started to plead, but the chief took out his watch. The pleading changed to cursing, but ended when Fellows, without looking up, raised a hand in preparation for a signal and Sergeant Unger came out from behind his desk to be ready. Hilders went to the door and said, "I'll go anywhere I want and talk to anybody I want in this town and you can't stop me." He slammed the door behind him as Fellows's arm came down.

The Hilders incident brought a laugh from the other newsmen, but it was the only laugh the day afforded. By the end of the afternoon five more identifications had fallen through, nothing had materialized in an hour of waiting outside Manny's restaurant, and the most likely firms had all been investigated. Another job change was uncovered, but the man didn't fit Campbell's description.

When Wednesday also passed without results, an air of gloom settled on headquarters. The men who had started Monday with enthusiasm induced by the novelty of the action and the expectation of results were now going through the motions of a distasteful job that had to be done with as little agony as possible. Questions were asked politely, but a deadness had crept into the policemen's tones. Watly was getting irritable at the frequent calls for his presence and his employer, Frank Restlin, was becoming irate. "How am I supposed to run a real estate office," he complained to Fellows on the phone, "when my man can't take prospective clients out to view the properties? How am I supposed to close deals when he keeps getting called away in the middle of them?"

Fellows said he didn't know, but it wouldn't last much longer. "After all, Mr. Restlin, we're trying to help you. You want to find the man who froze your pipes, don't you? You want the man who left a body in your house, don't you? A murder in your house hurts your business, doesn't it?"

"That doesn't hurt my business," Restlin retorted. "I got a lot of free advertising. What's hurting it is having my man hamstrung."

Even Sid Wilks was showing the effects. "You know

what's going to happen?" he said to Fellows when he
checked in late Wednesday afternoon.

"No, Sid. What?"

"Nothing. That's what. We're not going to find him.
We're going to wrap it up tomorrow and we're not going to find him."

"We still might."

"Don't kid yourself. We're scraping the bottom now.
All the likely places were covered the first two days. It's
what I've been telling you. You try to read too much
into your clues. The guy doesn't work in Stockford. You
just stretched your clues so fine you jump from one in-
tangible to another and you end up in outer space."

"He came there every night about five-thirty, Sid. I
don't think I'm reaching very far for my interpreta-
tion."

"It's still a reach, Fred. You jump to the conclusion
he comes from a job that gets out at five. He could
come from New Haven from a job that gets out at
four, or he could be a rich man's son who doesn't work
at all and picked five-thirty out of a hat. He could be
an artist or a writer who doesn't keep any hours. He
could be anything, Fred."

"He could, Sid, but the law of averages says it's more
likely what I've got."

"Well, you're going to have to get something else because, I can tell you, this isn't it."

When Wilks came in Thursday morning a man was sitting in Fellows's office trying not to look at the picture gallery. He was a medium-sized middle-aged man with a gray balding head, a pleasant face, and glasses. He smiled apologetically when the detective sergeant stuck his head in the door, and said, "Chief Fellows asked me to meet him here."

"Make yourself comfortable." Wilks backed out and when the chief came in, said, "What gives, Fred? Who's he?"

"His name is Bunnell. He's new in town."

"He got anything to do with the case?"

Fellows looked a little sheepish. "Yes, and if you think I reached in the stratosphere before, you'll think I'm out of the solar system now." He took off his coat and hat and hung them on the rack by the bulletin board with its schedule lists, rules and regulations, insurance company calendar, messages, and loose thumbtacks. "But hell, Sid," he said, "he's about all that's left."

The two went into the office, where Fellows introduced himself and the sergeant and thanked Mr. Bunnell for coming. "Mr. Bunnell," he explained to Wilks, "is the man Watly showed the house to the day before the robbery. You remember?"

"Yeah, I remember," Wilks said, looking sideways at the chief.

Fellows sat down in his chair and Wilks closed the door and leaned against it. "Now, Mr. Bunnell, it was the twenty-fifth of February that you went out to look at the house, wasn't it?"

"Yes, sir. It was."

"Would you tell us everything that happened?"

Bunnell scratched his ear. "Near as I can recall, Mr. Fellows. You see, I've recently taken a job here in town and my family and I were living temporarily in a furnished flat, but we wanted to get something of our own, something reasonable. I'm a school teacher and it was vacation. We'd gone to spend a few days with my folks and when we got back, I set about seeing what I could find. I went to the Restlin Agency and talked to Mr. Restlin and Mr. Watly about my needs, and Mr. Restlin thought he had just the place for me. He said it would be available the first of March and it was quite reasonable. It was furnished, but he felt some arrangement could be made if I wanted to use my own things and he told Mr. Watly to take me out and look at it. This was the middle of the afternoon, as I recall, and Mr. Watly said certainly.

"We went out in my car and it did look like the kind of place I wanted. There was quite a bit of ground around and I have three children, so it was fine on that score. We got out and it had an empty look about it, no sign of life, but we walked around to the back and he showed me the garage and where the property extended and I asked if we might see the inside. He thought the people there wouldn't have any objection and we rang the bell several times but there was no answer. He tried the door and it was locked. He didn't have any keys with him, so he said that perhaps if we came back the next day there'd be somebody home. I agreed because, while it looked like just what we wanted, I'd like to see the inside and I'd like to have my wife see it. We went back and talked to Mr. Restlin about it and it was left that I'd bring my wife with me the next afternoon and we'd take a look and they'd bring along keys, so if no one were home, we could go in and look around anyway.

"Of course, none of that happened. I went back the next day and Mr. Restlin was home and Mr. Watly was in a dither because of the body you people had discovered."

"Did you mention this to anyone, Mr. Bunnell?" Fellows was particularly interested in this angle. "How many people knew you were going to look at that house on Thursday?"

"Well, my wife, of course." He hesitated. "But if you mean knew it was that particular house, then I can't tell you. I told her about where it was and what it looked like and I guess I mentioned that we might have found a place to a couple of neighbors who knew we were looking."

"Would you give me the names of those neighbors, the ones you told?"

"I'm not sure which ones I did tell."

Fellows pulled a pad over. "Let me have the names of anybody you or your wife might have told, anybody at all. That would be that afternoon or early evening."

"Just Mrs. Curran, our landlady, and the Motts next door, Mr. and Mrs. Mott. And the Furlows down on the first floor. Those would be the only ones."

Fellows noted the names and wrote Bunnell's address beside them. "What do Mr. Mott and Mr. Furlow look like?"

"They're both elderly. Mr. Mott—"

"How old?"

"Oh, in their sixties, at least I should judge so."

"Never mind then. You're sure no one else could have known?"

"Quite sure."

Fellows thought a moment. "Did you see anyone around when you were looking at the house? In the woods, driving by, anything?"

Mr. Bunnell shook his head. "No. That's not to say there couldn't have been someone. But the whole place looked quite desolate and empty."

Fellows asked a few more brief questions and thanked the man and saw him to the door. Wilks watched the process like an adult observing a child's game. "And what," he said when the man had gone, "was the meaning of all that?"

Fellows sat down at the desk again. "Stealing the lease to conceal his handwriting sounds crazy, but it's really quite plausible when you get down to it. That I can understand. What I've never yet been able to figure is why Campbell quit and ran."

"We talked that over Saturday night."

"I know. And what it boils down to, of course, is fear of—no, not fear—expectation of discovery. He must have known or thought he would be interrupted."

Wilks sat against the table with his arms folded and smiled pityingly. "It could equally well be that he decided it was too much trouble and said the hell with it."

Fellows smiled back. He said, "If I were trying to cover up a murder, I don't think anything would be too much trouble."

Wilks shrugged. "A point for the defense. So Campbell thought he was going to be discovered. What makes you pick a possible client for a threat?"

"The fact that I can't find anything else. I made a trip out there yesterday. I asked Mrs. Banks if she ever smelled anything those nights before he left. She hadn't. I tried the other neighbors down the road. They didn't.

None of them had showed the slightest interest in Campbell or his house or what went on there. Nobody was going to call on them. I asked about the children in the neighborhood. Had they played around Campbell's place? They hadn't. The upshot of it was that no one around there knew anything about Campbell until we found the body. But he quit destroying the body and robbed the real estate office instead. That was Wednesday night. Obviously something was going to happen Thursday. I don't know what it could be except, possibly, that he knew Bunnell was coming."

Wilks said, "True, but there could be other reasons you don't know about."

"I can only work with what I know."

"And you know now that Campbell couldn't possibly have known Bunnell was coming, so where does that leave you?"

"With another bum lead. I'm used to it."

"It's that stratosphere stuff, Fred. If you'll note what's happened in this case, all the dead ends have come from following up conclusions based on conclusions based on conclusions, not from tracing real evidence."

Fellows shook his head. "I can't sell you on anything, can I?"

"Not me, Fred. Not that stratosphere stuff. The only thing that'll sell me is showing somebody to Watly today and having Watly say, 'That's the man,' only that's not going to happen, because it's another one of your conclusions." He went to the door and said sadly, "I'll bet all my cribbage losses, double or nothing, that we're going to finish the job this afternoon and it's going to be another dead end. I'll bet you Campbell doesn't work anywhere near Stockford."

Sergeant Wilks was right, at least on the first half of his bet. From one o'clock on the officers of the Stockford police force began drifting back into headquarters, their questioning assignments completed. Watly had been called out once that morning and breaths were held, but it was another false alarm and after that there was nothing. The last man reported in at five minutes of three, and Fellows, his desk piled high with their reports, was busy sorting and checking, making sure not one place had been overlooked. If he learned nothing about the murder, he learned a lot about the town. His face was solemn as he worked, but not disappointed. Having expected nothing, he had no reason to be.

Wilks came in, looking glum himself. He stared at the chief bent over his papers, and said, "You want some help with that, Fred?"

"No thanks, Sid. I'm sending all the others home. You might as well go home too."

"There's the Grafton Tool and Die Company, Fred. I suppose we could check it. They employ a thousand people."

"It's kind of far away."

"It's not the center of town, but a guy might get to Campbell's house from there in half an hour if he didn't buy more than a couple of things at the grocer's."

"It's something to look into, Sid. Maybe I'll line that up over the weekend."

"You don't sound as though it's the end of the world."

"There's still an angle or two left, Sid. We'll work them out."

"O.K. I'll see you in the morning."

Chief Fellows didn't show up for muster on Friday, March thirteenth. Sergeant Wilks stood in for him, calling the roll and reading out the day's assignments. On this day the assignments were all routine, traffic and beats. The murder case was out of it and there were no other problems that needed special attention.

Fellows himself came in at half past eight, half an hour after the force had gone out, and with him was a girl. "This is Jean Sherman," he said to Wilks, introducing them. "I think it's about time we got her into this again."

He brought her into his office with a puzzled Wilks following, then leaned out to say to Sergeant Unger, "Get hold of Watly, will you? Ask him to come over right away." He closed the door and seated Miss Sherman in his swivel chair.

Wilks said, "Don't tell me what this is all about. I only work here."

"It's more of my stratosphere stuff. It probably won't pay off, but by the law of averages, Sid, if you keep trying long enough, something's bound to happen."

"What's supposed to happen this time?"

"Figure it out. She and Watly are the only two people we know of who've seen Campbell."

"You're not going to have them draw another picture are you?"

"That's one possibility," Fellows admitted, "but I'm hoping just a little bit that we won't have to resort to that."

The girl sat quietly, a little bit awed, a little bit embarrassed. Wilks said to her, "Do you know what this is all about? I can see the chief won't tell me."

She shook her head. "He came this morning and got me out of bed. I don't know what it's for."

Wilks bit savagely into a hunk of chewing tobacco. The look he gave Fellows said it was more hocus-pocus.

At quarter of nine, Sergeant Unger opened the door. "Mr. Watly's here."

Fellows brightened. He went out to greet him. "Sorry, Mr. Watly. We're taking up a lot of your time."

Watly nodded. He had passed the stage of enjoying any of this. He had even passed the stage of complaining.

Fellows stood aside and let him enter the office first. Watly took one step inside the door.

In the chief's chair, Jean Sherman shrank back, then stumbled to her feet. Her voice was a shriek. "It's him! It's John Campbell!"

When Jean screamed, Wilks froze against the table, and Watly sagged against the wall, his face gray. Only Fellows seemed to know what he was doing. He shut the door and pulled out a chair. Jean moved into a corner, staring at Watly with a look akin to horror, her hand at her throat, her breasts rising and falling rapidly. Fellows took the stunned real estate man by the arm and aided him into the seat. "How about it, Mr. Watly?" he said. "You want to tell us about it?"

Watly leaned his elbows on the table and buried his face in his hands. "It's been driving me crazy. I haven't been able to sleep or eat for waiting." He looked up. "Let me explain," he begged. "I can explain everything if you'll only listen."

"We'll listen. You just wait here." He opened the door and ushered Jean Sherman out into the arms of a flabbergasted Sergeant Unger. He said, "Thank you very much, Miss Sherman. You've been a great help. Now, if you'll go with the sergeant, I'll have him take you upstairs and get your statement." He said to Unger, "First get Ed Lewis. I'm going to want him for Watly's confession."

Unger nodded and got busy. He departed with the

girl as Wilks came out of the office. The detective sergeant was eyeing Fellows suspiciously. He said, "Something tells me this wasn't pure accident, your bringing Watly and the girl together."

Fellows grinned and moved to the door where he could look in on Raymond Watly, who was resting his head on his hands. "I wanted to satisfy myself," he said to Wilks.

"You might prepare a guy for a shock like that. I'm not a young man any more."

"I couldn't, Sid. It was more of my stratosphere stuff and if I let on I suspected him and I was wrong again, I'd be the laughing stock of the town."

"How did you do it?"

"I added up my theories, Sid. We figured Campbell was married, that he worked in downtown Stockford, but lived in another town, one not too far away. We had him a salesman, one who worked regular hours in the daytime and did door-to-door selling at night. We also figured he didn't want us to have his handwriting because we could identify it, either because he had a jail record or because he was close by. We also felt he did have a record somewhere. And we thought he abandoned the body because he was sure of discovery —and the only certainty of discovery was by a prospect coming out to look at the house. That was all that stratosphere stuff you were talking about, and I expected to be wrong on a lot of it, but I couldn't see how I could be wrong on all of it. I just couldn't believe that.

"So then, thinking about this guy Bunnell, it occurred to me that the only guy who resembled Watly's description at all and who could have known Bunnell would go to the house was Watly himself. As soon as I thought of that, I realized that there was still one person who worked in Stockford Center who hadn't been cleared by Watly and that again was Watly himself. Of course I thought I was crazy, but then I began to think I wasn't crazy because more and more I could see everything fell into place if Watly was the guy. He's married. He works in Stockford, but he lives in Ashmun. He's in real estate. That's a selling job. And he was out the night you called him to go to Stamford with us. He could have gone to a movie, but he could also have been house-to-house selling, especially since his wife was home to say he was out. Then there were the differences in description, his and Jean Sherman's. He said Campbell was five-ten, two inches shorter than he was. Jean said he was six feet. Watly said Campbell wore better clothes than he could buy. Jean said they were average clothes. Watly had him wearing a tan overcoat. Jean said a dark coat. Watly wears a dark one." Fellows shrugged. "It'd have been rough if I'd been wrong this time. This was the last gasp."

Wilks looked in the office door and said, "Now it's only rough on Watly."

Ed Lewis reported in half an hour later, and the three policemen brought in chairs and sat with Watly around the small table. The real estate agent had been begging for someone to listen to his story about the terrible business with Joan Simpson and when they were ready and Lewis had his pad set, Fellows said, "All right, Watly. Now you can talk."

"It was a terrible thing," Watly said nervously. He was halting in his speech as he began, but grew more fluent as he unfolded his story. "I met Joan Simpson first when I was working for the Masters Toy Company in Bridgeport. She was the boss's secretary. I guess you'd call her his mistress."

Fellows said, "And you worked under the name John Lawrence, right?"

He nodded. "I read you found that out, but I don't know how. I mean how you knew Lawrence was Campbell."

"And you were fired for playing around. You been seeing her all this time?"

Watly shook his head. "I never saw her after. I don't mean she wasn't a nifty dish back then when she was only about twenty, but, well, she had a setup and she didn't want to risk it. I didn't bother trying to see her after I left the company."

"You married back then?"

Watly hesitated. Finally he nodded. "I don't want you to get the wrong idea. That has nothing to do with it."

"Nobody said it has."

"I mean—I don't want you to get wrong ideas about me. I know a husband isn't supposed to fool around, but I can't help it. I'm made that way. Please don't get prejudiced against me because of that."

"Go on with the story."

"Well, I didn't see Joan after that. That was, let's see, back in April of '51. I had to get another job. I got one selling beauty preparations door to door. Lady Alma. I still do."

"Calling yourself John Campbell or John Lawrence, or Raymond Watly?"

He wet his lips. "I call myself John Lawrence."

"You introduce yourself to your customers as John Lawrence? Is that how the company has you listed?"

"No. They know me as Raymond Watly."

"Which is your real name?"

"Raymond Watly. Raymond Kirk Watly."

"We'll straighten out this name business in a minute. First I want to know why you use the name Lawrence to your customers. Is that so they can't make complaints against you?"

"No, no. I don't do anything they'd complain about."

"Then it's so they can't trace you."

Watly was perspiring. "I don't want you to get the wrong idea, Chief. I don't want you prejudiced."

"I think you mean you don't want us to get the right

idea. What do you do, seduce your customers under the name of John Lawrence?"

"I—" He said, "Let me tell you the story, please."

"You ever been arrested, Watly?" When Watly didn't answer, the chief repeated the question.

"Can't I tell you the story?" Watly pleaded.

"We'll hear your story. I want to know your background. Have you ever been arrested?"

Watly nodded faintly.

"What for?"

"When I was about seventeen, I forged a check. The judge let me off with a warning. Then I was arrested for burglary, but I got let off. Then a couple of months later I was arrested for burglary again and got six months. When I got out, I got a job in a supermarket and then I got sent to jail for a year for embezzling eight hundred dollars." He said with the desperate need to be believed, "but that was when I was a kid. Honest, I never did anything after that. I left town and started over. I'd learned my lesson, believe me. The draft rated me 4-F, and I changed my name to John Lawrence and got a job in a war plant and I made good money and did fine. That was way back in 1944, and I've been straight ever since.

"After the war I was laid off when they cut back and I got a job in the sales department of a refrigerator plant for a couple of years and after that—"

"What happened? Why did you leave them?"

"I got fired."

"What for?"

"I got one of the girls in trouble."

"You ever been arrested on a morals charge?"

Watly shook his head vigorously. "No. Believe me. I never seduced young girls. I never got in trouble that way. I only got in trouble for being wild in my youth, but that's over long ago. Listen, I'm square now. In fact, I'm chairman of our local United Fund drive. I'm an honest man. I've been chairman two years running and I've never touched a penny."

"All right, Mr. Watly. Let's get back to your getting fired."

"Well, that was in 1947 and I got a job in the sales department of a bakery in a new town. I was still using the name John Lawrence. The next year, that was 1948, I got married. Of course I told my wife about myself and we got married under my real name and that's what she called me, but I was still working with the other name. Then, in 1949 I quit the baking company—I didn't get fired, I had a better offer. That was from the toy company where I met Joan. I had to work there under the name Lawrence, but when I got fired and got the beauty preparation job, my wife wanted me to use my real name and I did and I've used that ever since in my work. She wanted me to because we were going to have a baby and she didn't want all that business and I was honest now and I thought nobody'd know I was an ex-con, so it'd be all right.

"Then, after the baby was born, I needed more money, so I took a part-time job for a while on the side, but then our other daughter was born and I quit the part-time job to take a full time job as a car salesman and I sold beauty preparations at night. I was doing all right and we bought a home in Ashmun and I commuted to the job, but that got pretty rugged, driving from Ashmun to Bridgeport every day, so I quit and started out in the real estate business in Ashmun. I wasn't doing as well as I wanted so a year later, when Mr. Restlin offered to take me in here, I went to work for him."

"When was that?"

"In August of 1957. I've been with him a year and a half."

"Let's get back to Joan Simpson."

"Yes, but meeting her was accidental." He covered

his face with his hands briefly. "That was a real bad accident! What happened was I called at her place one night selling Lady Alma stuff. She had a couple of roommates, but they were out and we struck up our old acquaintance again. After that I saw quite a bit of her. At first it was fun, like we used to have, and when I'd have time or when I was selling around Townsend and felt like some excitement, I'd call up and see her. The trouble was, she'd changed. I didn't know it at first, but along about the end of last summer it was getting obvious. She was starting to make demands on me and she was starting to talk about marriage. It hadn't been like that before. When she was young she didn't care about marriage. Now, the first thing I knew she was talking divorce and me marrying up with her. And more than that, she was telling me when her roommates would be out so I could see her. She was expecting things.

"So, I wasn't going to put up with that. I quit coming around. That was November or December sometime but the trouble was, when I first ran into her, I let down my hair a little for old times' sake and told her I lived in Ashmun. When I stopped seeing her, she made inquiries of the Lady Alma company. She found out there was no John Lawrence working there, but she learned a Raymond Watly lived in Ashmun and that did it. One day in January, damned if I don't come home and find her in front of the house waiting for me. She'd taken the bus over and I quick took her for a ride around and drove her home and tried to set her straight that the whole thing was no go. She wouldn't listen to me. First she pleaded, then she threatened. She said she'd go to my wife if I didn't see her. So I saw her again and she kept after me. She said we were right for each other and I needed her and she wanted to prove it. She said the only way she could prove it was for us to live together as man and wife. I didn't want that, but she wouldn't listen to reason and I was scared she'd go to my wife and I finally gave in. I thought maybe the best way to make her leave me alone was to go along with it. I figured after a month or so she'd be satisfied."

Fellows said, "You had her believing it was for three months."

Watly was momentarily flustered. Then he said, "Well, she wanted it for three months and I agreed, but I only rented the house for one month. I thought that would be enough to convince her. If it wasn't, then I could renew the lease." He glanced around the circle of faces, trying to measure the amount of feeling against him.

"I rented the house in the name of John Campbell because, of course, I couldn't let anybody know it was me. This was all right with her and she called herself Joan Campbell."

"So you set her up in a house and came to see her."

"Yes, sir. I told my wife I was going out selling as usual, but I couldn't sell. She made me come see her every night and one night, one Friday, she insisted that I come for dinner. She bought the things herself and made a big fancy production and I had to come to it because if I didn't do what she said, she'd tell my wife. So I had that dinner with her and I brought her groceries the other nights after work and I came to see her every evening but still that didn't satisfy her. The next thing I knew she wanted me to spend a weekend with her. She said it wasn't like being married when I didn't stay overnight so I had to tell my wife I was going away on business for a weekend and I went there.

"That was a Friday night. That was February twentieth. That was the night I decided I couldn't stand it any longer. We had a fight. I told her it was the end, that even if she went to my wife I wasn't going to go on with it. So she got very angry and she grabbed a carving knife out of the kitchen and came at me." He buried his face. "I didn't know she was going to do this, otherwise I would have run. But she came at me and I tried to get out of the way and I stumbled and fell over backwards and she was rushing at me so hard that she tripped over me and fell against the fireplace and hit her head."

Watly looked up with a tortured expression. "I thought she was just knocked unconscious. I put the knife back and carried her into the bedroom, but I couldn't revive her and then I examined her and found out she was—dead." He put his face in his hands again. "She'd hit her head and done something and she was dead."

He looked up pleadingly. "You've got to believe me. I didn't know what to do. At first I was going to call the police and then I realized how bad it'd make me look, the way we were living and all, and there weren't any witnesses. Everybody would think I was guilty no matter what I said. I tore my hair out wondering what to do."

"And you decided to go to New York," Fellows said with a trace of sarcasm.

"I had to get away where I could think. I didn't want to go home because then I'd have to explain why I'd come back. Besides, my wife would know something was wrong. I had to get away—far away. So that's what I did. I banked the furnace and locked the room and the house and drove to the station for the first train to New York."

"And made a date with Miss Sherman."

Watly rubbed his face. "I know that sounds terrible, but you don't understand. I knew I was going to have to do something about Joan's body, but I couldn't face up to it. I wanted companionship."

"Not your wife's, of course."

"You don't understand. I wanted an uncomplicated

relationship. I just wanted to be with a woman. It's always been that way with me. When I'm in trouble, I turn to a woman. That's why I went to New York and that's why I started that thing with Jean. She would have been nice for the weekend, but she was busy and I brought her back with me because, somehow, it wouldn't seem quite so terrible going back into that house if she were with me.

"We just spent that one night and I put her on the nine o'clock train the next morning and went to work. Mr. Restlin wasn't there because he usually takes Mondays off. He keeps the office open seven days a week because weekends and holidays and times like that are good. That's when people go out house-hunting. I don't work weekends, so he does and he takes Mondays off. That meant I didn't have to face him with all that terrible thing on my mind. I'd decided the best thing to do was try to dispose of her body if I possibly could and the thing I decided to do was burn it in the furnace.

"I went out there that night. That was Monday night. It was a terrible night for me. It was the worst thing I ever had to do in my life. I cut her up in the bathtub, her arms and legs, and I took them down in a bushel basket I lined with newspapers and burned them in the furnace and then I just couldn't go on. I left her in the bathtub and locked up the house and went home. The nightmares I had!"

He rubbed his agonized face briefly. The men around him stared stonily. "Then I went out again Tuesday night and the house was cold. I was so upset the night before I forgot to bank the furnace and the fire was out. I didn't want to waste time trying to start it again. I'm not good at coal furnaces. It took me all afternoon to get it going the day before Joan moved in and I didn't want to try it again. So I built a big fire in the fireplace and that's where I burned her head and that's

all I did that night because it smelled so terribly. I came
home again and I decided the next night I'd start the
furnace again only that was the day that man Bunnell
wanted to look at the house.

"I'd left it locked and we couldn't get in, but I was
desperately afraid Mr. Restlin would take him back
there with a key. Fortunately we talked about it on the
way back to the office and I influenced him and he
decided he'd wait till the next day and bring his wife.

"I couldn't wait any longer and I knew I wouldn't
have time to get rid of the whole body in one night,
having to build a fire in the furnace and all. It'd take
so long my wife would want to know what was the
matter. I was supposed to be out selling and I couldn't
come home late without her asking questions. So I put
the body in the trunk in the cellar and packed all her
things, only I didn't know what to do with her suitcases. I didn't want to take them with me, so I left
them. I thought maybe I'd be able to come back after
Bunnell saw the house, but when I got there, the smell
was still around and I was sure the whole thing would
be found out and the first thing the police would do
would be to check the lease and it was signed in my
handwriting. So I went down to the office without
turning on the lights and took all the leases and then
punched a hole in the glass in the door and left." He
looked up. "I wasn't trying to be a burglar. I guess I
did the wrong things all around, but you've got to understand how frightened I was. I wasn't able to think
straight. All I wanted to do was get rid of the body
and pretend I didn't know anything about it. And
when I did all that and burned the leases in the fireplace when I got home, I was sure I'd get caught. You
kept coming around to see me and get me in on things
and I was afraid I was going to give myself away every
time I opened my mouth." Watly paused, staring fear-
fully at the chief. Fellows shook his head. "You didn't

have to worry about that, Mr. Watly. You were very convincing."

"I was desperate, Mr. Fellows. I knew it'd be all up with me if you caught me. I knew it would look bad. I was afraid I wouldn't be able to convince you I was innocent."

When Watly was through with his story, silence reigned for a moment. Fellows was playing with his key chain, matching keys together, separating them and evening them up again. At length he said without looking up, "Most of what you told us, I guess, is true, Mr. Watly. But that part about her coming at you with a knife— that part, I think, is a lie."

Watly, white-faced, said, "Every word is true. I told it exactly as it happened."

"Mr. Watly, I think you killed her. You killed her because she told you she was going to have a baby. You didn't burn just her head and limbs, you also destroyed some of her internal organs."

"She didn't tell me that, I swear it. She wasn't going to have a baby. It was in the papers, so you know that's true. She never said it."

"You still destroyed those organs."

"I wasn't trying to hide anything. I had finished with the other parts and I was starting in on the body. I just happened to start there."

The chief raised his eyes. "You say you didn't kill her, but you bought a knife and a hacksaw. You purchased them at Cutler's Hardware store. We traced them there."

"I know that. I admit that, but I didn't buy them before she died, I bought them afterwards."

"When?"

"I bought them—let's see—Monday." He reaffirmed it. "I put Jean Sherman on the train and then I bought the saw and knife. That hardware store is near the station. That's why I bought them there."

Fellows shook his head. "I don't believe you, Mr. Watly. I think you bought them there before Monday."

"I wasn't near the station before Monday. I wouldn't have bought them near the station if I hadn't been taking Jean to the train."

"You'd buy them there because it's out of the way. You work in this town. You wouldn't shop where you might be known."

"I swear it. She fell and hit her head. I bought them Monday."

Fellows exhaled. "All right, Mr. Watly. Now we'll go over your story again. You tell us the whole thing all over again, just what you did and what she did. And you might start with that lease you signed. Where'd you get the name Campbell and the Gary Hardware Company?"

"I made up the name Campbell and I remembered the Gary Hardware Company from ads I'd seen. I told Joan, so if anybody asked she'd say I worked in hardware."

"That's a lot of scheming to hide a love affair, Watly. It makes better sense if you admit you planned to kill her right along."

"I didn't," he pleaded. "I bought the saw and knife after she died. I only bought them when I decided to destroy her body."

"What did you do with her belongings, the things that might identify her for us?"

"I burned them. I burned everything I could."

"You didn't burn the house down. Why didn't you do that?"

Watly was a real estate man. He looked at the chief in real surprise. "Burn down a house?" He shook his head. "I never even thought of such a thing."

"And you told your wife you were going away for the weekend, but you didn't actually get home until Monday night."

"I called her from New York after Jean said she'd meet me. I said I'd be held up an extra day."

"And she didn't question it?"

"No. Why should she? I'm an honest man." He leaned forward. "You're holding it against me because I made some mistakes in my youth. You're holding it against me because I play around. You're holding it against me because I had a woman back to the house. I admit that looks bad, but that doesn't make me a murderer." He raised his voice. "I didn't kill her!"

"All right. Let's have the whole thing all over again."

"Why? I told it to you once."

"Tell it to us again."

Watly did. He related the whole story, only this time he was interrupted with question after question by Fellows. Despite the jarring effect of the chief, he made no changes, he didn't trip himself. She had rushed at him with a knife, tripped, and struck her head.

"There was no mark on the fireplace where you say she hit it."

"Then she didn't leave any mark, but that's what she did."

"What kind of a knife was she waving at you?"

"A long kitchen knife, like a carving knife. I don't remember it exactly."

"You put it back. You ought to remember it. What's the knife look like?"

"A wood-handled knife. That's all I remember."

"It was the knife you bought at Cutler's, wasn't it?"

"No! I didn't buy that knife until Monday."

"Go on."

When he had told it a second time, he was made to

tell it again and this time Wilks as well as Fellows kept interrupting, kept quizzing him on major points and minor details. It came out the same way.

At noon they took a break for lunch, having it served in the office, and then they went at it again and still again, always with the same result. He wouldn't be shaken on his claim that she had rushed at him in a rage, fallen headlong against the brick fireplace, and dropped dead.

By four o'clock Watly was hoarse. They were all hoarse. They paused and Watly was nearly in tears and nervous prostration, but he clung to his story with an earnestness that was pathetic and, because it was pathetic, it was convincing. But Fellows and Wilks wouldn't be convinced.

They gave up finally and had him put in a cell. Sergeant Gorman and one of the patrolmen locked him in and Ed Lewis departed to type up the statement for the real estate agent's signature. Fellows and Wilks stayed behind in the office and their frustration was evident.

"The trouble is," Wilks complained bitterly, "we can't prove otherwise."

"I don't care how often he denies it, he killed her. I'd bet my life on it."

"What good does the betting do? We're over a barrel. He doesn't have to prove he didn't murder her, we have to prove he did. We don't have a chance."

Fellows said irritably, "Don't be silly, Sid. Of course we have a chance."

"Show me where. How did she die? Nobody knows. It could have been an accident like he says. As for the knife and saw, Cutler's has no record. How're we going to prove he bought them Friday, or before that even? It could have been Monday like he says. We have our version of what happened and he has his. The only trouble is, we have to prove ours."

Fellows's voice was snappish. "All right, Sid. You don't have to tell me all that. I'm not stupid."

"A brilliant job of catching the guy and then we can't touch him—all because a lousy hardware store doesn't keep records."

"All right, Sid. Cut it out." Fellows got to his feet and threw open the door, stalking into the main room. Gorman, at the desk, said, "I just got a call from a reporter on Watly. I confirmed it."

"The hell with the reporters."

"They're going to be coming here."

Fellows ignored him and stood with his hands on his hips, glowering at the steel door to the cell block. Wilks walked slowly out of the office and leaned against the door frame, watching the chief. Fellows growled in unaccustomed anger. "This damned place looks like a pigsty. Look at the dust in the corners. Sweep this place up, Gorman."

The tone of Fellows's voice was so foreign to his nature that Gorman said quickly, "Yes, sir," and jumped to obey. The chief said, "And empty those ash trays. Clean up this place. Goddamn it, what are we running here?" He jammed his hands in his pockets and his eyes searched out the room for more omissions. His voice came up sharply again, but this time there was a different note in it. "And who's the sloppy guy in charge of this office? It's March. It's the thirteenth day of March. What's February still doing on the calendar?" He stalked to the bulletin board and tore off the offending sheet, but the vengeance of his action wasn't quite like the anger he'd shown before. He came back, folding the sheet into uneven quarters and thrust it at Gorman. "Here," he snapped. "Never mind the broom. Take this in to Watly. Tell him it's a present from me."

Gorman said another quick, "Yes, sir," and hastened to obey. He hurried for the keys, hastened to unlock the door, and went quickly down the concrete corridor. Sidney Wilks, watching the performance, moved up beside the chief and looked sideways at the glint in Fellows's eyes. He jerked his head after the retreating sergeant and said, "What's all that big act for?"

Fellows's face broke into a sly grin. "You know something, Sid? I'm a lousy detective. I don't know when I'd've caught on if I hadn't looked at that calendar. Monday, the twenty-third of February, the day Watly claims he bought the knife? That's in red numbers. It's a legal holiday. The stores were closed."

From the cell at the end of the hall there came the sudden sound of sobbing.

FINE MYSTERY AND SUSPENSE TITLES FROM CARROLL & GRAF

☐ Bentley, E.C./TRENT'S OWN CASE $3.95
☐ Blake, Nicholas/MURDER WITH MALICE $3.95
☐ Blake, Nicholas/A TANGLED WEB $3.50
☐ Boucher, Anthony/THE CASE OF THE
    BAKER STREET IRREGULARS $3.95
☐ Boucher, Anthony (ed.)/FOUR AND
    TWENTY BLOODHOUNDS $3.95
☐ Brand, Christianna/DEATH IN HIGH HEELS $3.95
☐ Brand, Christianna/FOG OF DOUBT $3.50
☐ Brand, Christianna/TOUR DE FORCE $3.95
☐ Brown, Fredric/THE LENIENT BEAST $3.50
☐ Brown, Fredric/MURDER CAN BE FUN $3.95
☐ Brown, Fredric/THE SCREAMING MIMI $3.50
☐ Browne, Howard/THIN AIR $3.50
☐ Buchan, John/JOHN MACNAB $3.95
☐ Buchan, John/WITCH WOOD $3.95
☐ Burnett, W.R./LITTLE CAESAR $3.50
☐ Butler, Gerald/KISS THE BLOOD OFF
    MY HANDS $3.95
☐ Carr, John Dickson/THE BRIDE OF
    NEWGATE $3.95
☐ Carr, John Dickson/CAPTAIN
    CUT-THROAT $3.95
☐ Carr, John Dickson/DARK OF
    THE MOON $3.50
☐ Carr, John Dickson/DEADLY HALL $3.95
☐ Carr, John Dickson/DEMONIACS $3.95
☐ Carr, John Dickson/THE DEVIL IN VELVET $3.95
☐ Carr, John Dickson/THE EMPEROR'S
    SNUFF-BOX $3.50
☐ Carr, John Dickson/FIRE, BURN! $3.50
☐ Carr, John Dickson/IN SPITE OF THUNDER $3.50
☐ Carr, John Dickson/LOST GALLOWS $3.50
☐ Carr, John Dickson/MOST SECRET $3.95
☐ Carr, John Dickson/NINE WRONG
    ANSWERS $3.50
☐ Carr, John Dickson/PAPA LA-BAS $3.95

- [ ] Hughes, Dorothy B./THE FALLEN SPARROW $3.50
- [ ] Hughes, Dorothy B./IN A LONELY PLACE $3.50
- [ ] Hughes, Dorothy B./RIDE THE PINK HORSE $3.95
- [ ] Innes, Hammond/ATLANTIC FURY $3.50
- [ ] Innes, Hammond/THE LAND GOD GAVE TO CAIN $3.50
- [ ] Kitchin, C. H. B./DEATH OF HIS UNCLE $3.95
- [ ] Kitchin, C. H. B./DEATH OF MY AUNT $3.50
- [ ] L'Amour, Louis/THE HILLS OF HOMICIDE $2.95
- [ ] Lewis, Norman/THE MAN IN THE MIDDLE $3.50
- [ ] MacDonald, John D./TWO $2.50
- [ ] MacDonald, Philip/THE RASP $3.50
- [ ] Mason, A.E.W./AT THE VILLA ROSE $3.50
- [ ] Mason, A.E.W./THE HOUSE OF THE ARROW $3.50
- [ ] Priestley, J.B./SALT IS LEAVING $3.95
- [ ] Queen, Ellery/THE FINISHING STROKE $3.95
- [ ] Rogers, Joel T./THE RED RIGHT HAND $3.50
- [ ] 'Sapper'/BULLDOG DRUMMOND $3.50
- [ ] Siodmak, Curt/DONOVAN'S BRAIN $3.50
- [ ] Symons, Julian/BLAND BEGINNING $3.95
- [ ] Symons, Julian/BOGUE'S FORTUNE $3.95
- [ ] Symons, Julian/THE BROKEN PENNY $3.95
- [ ] Wainwright, John/ALL ON A SUMMER'S DAY $3.50
- [ ] Wallace, Edgar/THE FOUR JUST MEN $2.95
- [ ] Waugh, Hillary/SLEEP LONG, MY LOVE $3.95
- [ ] Willeford, Charles/THE WOMAN CHASER $3.95

Available from fine bookstores everywhere or use this coupon for ordering.